INFERNAL

BY

DAUZED MELGAREJO JR.

This book is a work of fiction. Places, events, and situations in this story are purely fictional. Any resemblance to actual persons, living or dead, is coincidental.

Artist of Front Cover, Jennifer Torres

ISBN: 1-4033-1928-6 (E-book)
ISBN: 1-4033-1929-4 (Paperback)

This book is printed on acid free paper.

1st Books - rev. 02/26/03

I thank God for giving me the
imagination to create
And to share what my mind has to
offer. Also for
Presenting me with the following
people who
Helped me achieve my dream:
Neil Baldwin, Martha Burns, Danielle
Capawanna
Maria & Mark Burgaleta-Larson,
Kristina, Sapna
Jennifer, to my family & friends, thank
you.
To my loving wife whose support did
Not allow me to abandon my dreams
And has always
Believed in me. To my parents and
sisters who always
Said to have confidence in myself,
Thank you.

THE WORLD THAT DWELLS WITHIN MY MIND IS AS DEEP AS AN OCEAN AND AS DARK AS ANY DREAM...

DAUZED MELGAREJO, JR.

AN UNPLEASANT FEELING AWAKENS ME. I HEAR SOMEONE CALLING ME, ***"HEY OVER HERE."*** I SIT UP ON MY BED LOOKING FOR THE VOICE THAT CALLS OUT TO ME. THE LIGHT OF THE MOON LIGHTS MY ROOM. I TURN TO MY LEFT FRIGHTENED BY THE IMAGE THAT I SEE WITHIN THE MIRROR. I CLOSE MY EYES PRAYING DEEP INSIDE OF ME HOPING THAT WHEN I OPEN MY EYES THE IMAGE THAT I SEE IS GONE. I OPEN MY EYES ONCE AGAIN; THE DEMON IS AN IMAGE OF MYSELF. I LIE BACK IN MY BED. THE DARKNESS IN MY ROOM SLOWLY DROWNS THE LIGHT OF THE MOON.

PEACE TO THE MIND OF THOSE WHO SUFFER THEIR OWN HELL...

I FEEL LOCKED TRAPPED WITHIN THE WALLS OF MY MIND. I FEEL CAST AWAY FROM THE GATES OF HEAVEN. I LOOK AROUND, LOST, NO WHERE TO GO, NO ONE TO HELP ME WITH THE QUESTIONS I HAVE OF WHY? WHY MY LIFE FEELS LIKE IT'S BEING STIRRED. I FEEL MY LIFE SPINNING AND CONFUSED. THEN EVERYTHING STOPS, SILENT. I SEE MY PARENTS AS THEY PASS BY. I YELL OUT, ***"MOTHER, FATHER!"*** I REACH OUT FOR THEM WITH TEARS IN MY EYES. THE GIANT DOORS THAT STAND BEFORE ME OPEN. THEY WALK IN AND SLOWLY FADE INTO THE MIST. ***"GOD!"*** I SCREAM OUT, ***"I'M KNOCKING AT YOUR DOOR. PLEASE SAVE ME FROM THOSE WHO SEEK MY MIND".*** I PAUSE FOR A MOMENT LIFT MY HAND AND NOTICE MY KNUCKLES BLEEDING. I LOOK UP AND SEE HEAVEN'S DOORS STAINED WITH MY BLOOD. MY EARS FILL WITH LAUGHTER. VOICES SCREAM OUT IN MADNESS, ***"KNOCK, KNOCK!"*** I SLOWLY SIT IN FRONT OF THOSE TALL MONSTEROUS DOORS. I LOOK AT THEM LIKE TWO GIANT BODIES. THEIR BACKS ARE FACING ME. I WEEP, I DESIRE SO MUCH TO OPEN THEM AND RUN THROUGH. I WANT TO FEEL AT PEACE. I CLOSE MY EYES BEGGING DEEP WITHIN MY SOUL, ***"PLEASE OPEN BEFORE THEY GET ME, PLEASE, RELEASE ME FROM THIS DREADFUL FEELING THAT TORMENTS ME."*** THE FEAR OF THEM WITH EVERY

BLINK OF AN EYE, THEY DRAW CLOSER AND CLOSER, I FEEL HUNTED. I LEAN MY HEAD OVER GENTLY RESTING IT ON MY KNEES. I KNOW THEY'RE DRAWING NEAR. HOPE SLOWLY FADES. I CLOSE MY EYES AND WAIT TILL THE END.....

IN A DARK ROOM LIT ONLY BY A DESK LAMP, A YOUNG WOMAN WEEPS...

YESTERDAY IS GONE. AS IT BECOMES ASHES
BEFORE MY EYES. I STAND AT THE DOOR OF
TOMORROW.

?

WHAT WILL TOMORROW HOLD? A QUESTION
WITH THOUGHT. DESTINY, YOU ARE
EVERYONE'S
MYSTERY.

A young man sits in his study writing in his journal. Tear drops fall on the pages as he writes, ***"Come into a world where angels cry, where rainbows reflect their dark colors, where demons are angels and angels are demons. You sit between heaven and hell. Shadows chase your mind, you run into a room where life is played like a chess game."*** The room is painted black and white like a checkerboard. Dreams burn like candles. Strange faces laugh at your confusion, their laughter echo throughout the canyons of your mind. You enter another room where there is a long hallway of a thousand doors to choose from. Choose wisely, it holds the fate of your sanity. But you must hurry, ***"Time is getting hotter than a pot of curry."*** You feel something creeping all over you. You hear voices of those haunting your dreams; wolves running after your innocence, you run. You hide. Your heart pounds with fear you look up to the sky praying for hope while you watch a star fall from grace. You sleep without a sound. You wake by shattered sounds that echo throughout the darkness.

In the horizon, the moon begins to climb. It has been so long since you have not seen the sunshine. You feel that you are sinking deeper into the earth. Cold chills run through you: You see shadows mocking your tears. Voices torment your mind, you scream, no sound comes out of your mouth. You see yourself sitting at a long table, to your right is God to your left is Satan. You drink from their cups and laughter fills your ears. You run and run but you can not escape. You feel yourself spinning. The world twirls around like a whirlpool. The tracks of lost souls footprints are left to remember what once was, ***What was?*** " You ask, ***"Is this a dream within a dream"***, you sit. You wonder. You are lost! There is no beginning or end. This is the world that God has forgotten, the incomplete creation. A lost world that my tormented mind has brought to life... A young woman walks out of the kitchen towards the bottom of the stairs and calls out to the young man, "Glenn honey?" He slowly turns his head towards the sound of her voice...

II
II
II II II II II II
II
II
II
II
II

PEACE
TO
THE
MIND

In a loft, there is a young man in a wheelchair rolling himself across the room. He passes a table that has picture frames on it. All of them face down but one, one of him hugging a beautiful young woman, but the glass of the frame is cracked. He comes to a window on the other side of the loft. As he reaches the window he stops and watches the city below him. He turns toward the sun in the far horizon. Forcing his eyes, he stares into the sun. His eyes begin to water blinded by the intensity of the light. A bottle of pills drop to the floor and spill followed by a bottle of Jack Daniels. As the shattering of the bottle echoes, he sees himself standing in the middle of the city street. He stands with his eyes closed, feeling the warm breeze against his face. Slowly he opens his eyes. He looks up toward the sky. The sky above him rapidly moves like someone was fast-forwarding a video. As he looks down, he realizes he is standing. He leans forward reaching for his legs and begins to feel them. He smiles. He cannot believe that he can actually feel the sensation of his hands on his legs. A flock of birds disperse over him. Suddenly, he hears a window glass shattering. He looks up and sees glass falling down upon him. He lifts his arms to cover himself but no glass falls on him. He is startled by a frightening scream followed by multiple voices. The young man looks up in front of him, he sees dark images approaching him rapidly; they crises-cross each other. They approach him… He notices their heads viciously rattling out of control like the tail of a rattlesnake. He quickly turns and runs toward a building. He runs up the stairs not knowing where to go. After a few flights of stairs, he pauses for a moment. He looks over the banister. There is nothing below him but the empty stairwell. Suddenly, he hears tormented screams as he notices on the next flight of steps a door. He quickly runs up to it. He opens the door and runs in turning to see if they are still behind him. Slowly he sees them creeping up the steps silently. Their heads rattle, then stopping with a violent blur. He watches as they creep over the last step. The young man quickly slams the door. He holds it with his body. Behind it he can hear them moving. Slowly, he walks away from the door looking around the room in fear. He notices that the room is his own. Against the wall on the other end of the room, he notices a man. The man is himself with his eyes closed and his arms spread apart hitting his head against the wall. He suddenly opens his eyes, runs across the loft and jumps out the window.

Shocked by what just happened he slowly walks across the room towards the shattered window, behind him he can hear the shadows whispering angrily, ***"Join us Jacob, join us"***, over and over. Jacob looks behind him towards the door. They are laughing and teasing him saying, ***"We are going to get you Jacob, we are going to take you to Hell!!"*** He turns and looks out the window. He notices a cathedral. He sees himself walking past the front steps of the church. A priest invites him in with a smile. He sees himself turn and ignore the priest. As he walks away, Jacob hears the priest say, ***"Jacob I am here to help you!"*** The priest disappointed turns and walks up the steps. Jacob looks to his left and sees the shadows running towards the priest. Jacob looks at the priest who looks up toward him and smiles. Jacob screams out to the priest trying to warn him about the shadows approaching him from behind, ***"Hey, run, run. Look behind you!"*** Pounding upon the window Jacob watches slowly as the shadows viciously attack the priest without mercy. The priest's blood drips down the cathedral's steps as they tear him apart. His screams echo in Jacob's head. He turns around, covering his ears with his hands and closes his eyes. Jacob falls to his knees trying to block out the screams. Suddenly, there is silence. He opens his eyes. Cautiously he uncovers his ears and looks around. He slowly gets up from his knees and looks out the window. Upon the cathedral's steps there is no sign of the priest.

There is a sudden loud bang like the slamming of an iron door behind him, Jacob turns and there she is Linda, his girlfriend.

Jacob calls out to her, ***"Linda?"*** He is surprised to see her standing in the middle of the room dressed in white with her eyes closed. Jacob looks at how beautiful she looks. He reminisces to when they were together. Jacob is interrupted by a violent memory flash of Linda and him having an argument. He grabs her by the neck, she screams. There is a sound of a car crash, rippling in his mind. Jacob takes a step towards her and suddenly her eyes open. Jacob is stunned and frightened by what he sees. Linda's head slowly begins to rattle violently as her head shakes harder and faster. She releases a dreadful scream. Jacob suddenly feels dizzy and the room around him begins to spin. She raises her arms to Jacob. Her head stops shaking and she says to him with a weeping voice, ***"Why Jacob, I've always been there for you, been there for you..."*** She repeats this over and over, ***"Been there for you, been there for you."*** Jacob, disoriented, walks away from her. He turns around and behind him the sound of her voice torments him. He covers his ears. The shadows behind the door begin to laugh saying, ***"We're going to get you. Jacob there is no escape from the Hell that awaits you."*** As they laugh, Jacob walks towards the bathroom dragging his feet. He sees someone inside. He holds onto the wall. At the entrance of the bathroom, he hears behind him the voice of Linda repeating over and over, ***"For you, been there for you, been there for you."*** Jacob looks over the edge of the door, he realizes it's him in a wheelchair, facing a mirror. He stands behind himself looking down on his own image in the wheelchair. Jacob lifts his head to the mirror. He sees his eyes are swollen with tears. Jacob moves out of the center of the room. He stands looking at himself. Jacob screams out loud with rage throwing his arms in the air. ***"Oh God! Why?"*** The shadows behind the door mock Jacobs cries. They laugh at him calling out his name, ***"Jacob..."***

Fatigued, he looks down on himself. Jacob's body is haggard wanting all this to end. He notices his other self, looking at him with a cold stare as the other's scream out. He raises his right hand and in it was a gun. He points it to his head and presses the trigger. Behind the blast you hear, ***"Been there for you"*** repeatedly, louder and louder.

Suddenly he sits up again and fires at his head. Jacob repeats this continuously. The blast gets louder and louder! The words, ***"Been there for you"*** become an agony to Jacob's ears. The room begins to spin faster and faster. Jacob screams! He opens his eyes as his face is filled with sweat, breathing heavily.

Silence surrounds him. The only sound he hears is the pounding of his heart. He looks down on himself while he's sitting in his wheelchair. He turns towards the window and looks at the floor, he notices that there was the shattered Jack Daniels bottle and next to it his scattered pills! Jacob turns to the mirror in front of him. He looks deep into it as it grew dark behind him. There are dark images coming towards him. As the images draw closer, he realizes that they are demons! The room begins to fill with screams and within the piercing cries is Linda's voice repeating over and over, ***"Been there for!!!*** Her voice grows louder and angrier.

In a whispering voice he hears, ***It's time!!*** Jacob leans forward feeling anguished and tormented. He leans back on his chair. He lifts his head and opens his eyes. When he turns his head he sees squatting next to him against the corner wall a demonic image of himself looking straight at him, chuckling. Jacob feels something-wet dripping down his face. He touches it. When he looks at his hand, he sees blood! He feels his head and touches the wound. Jacob feels cold and his eyes grow glassy and lifeless. He screams and his anguish are silenced by a gunshot!

I seek for peace.

I seek for salvation.

I seek for angels.

I've read books of people that have seen angels. People that had been saved by angels, when they came close to a near death experience or fell into dark troubled times. Those who came across these angels felt a calm presence of peace and tranquility.

I seek for peace.

I seek for salvation.

I seek for heaven

Why do I only see demons?

Why do I fear?

Why do I live in hell?

Where are my angels to save me from my tomorrow?

In a room lying in a bed a man sleeps. He wakes up fully absorbed in sweat breathing heavily from a bad dream. He is sitting in his bed with tears in his eyes. Out side his window he hears the sound of his neighbor's dog howling and releasing a low moan. He gently gets out of bed and walks into his daughter's room where she sleeps. He opens the door and peaks in. He sees her siting up on her bed looking back at him. She says to him softly, ***"Dad what's wrong?"***

He walks in and says, ***"Nothing baby, why are you up?"***

"I can't sleep", responds his daughter.

He walks over to her and tucks her into bed.

She says to him, ***"Dad you're sweating, did you have a bad dream?"***

He answers, ***"Yeah."***

She puts her hands on her father's face and says to him, ***"Don't worry Dad everything will be okay. I love you!"***

He reaches out to her and hugs her. His daughter hugs him back and he says to her, ***"I love you too!"*** She holds him tight and lies back in bed, closing her eyes.

He stands, walks to the door and says, ***"You're going to be 12 years old and guess what? I'm going to take you to Adventure Park!"***

Excited, she says smiling, ***"Yeah! Cool, that's awesome, thanks Dad!"***

As he shuts off the lights and closes the door he says, ***"Good night baby."***

She responds, ***"Good night Dad."***

Before closing the door completely he hears his daughter saying in a sweet voice words of encouragement and comfort for a father who dreads to sleep and wake someday to see his nightmares become reality.

She calls out to him before he walks away, ***"Dad?"***

He turns and opens the door saying, ***"Yeah baby?"***

"No more bad dreams", she says.

He smiles saying, ***"Yeah, no more bad dreams."***

He closes the door and walks down the hall. He looks back to his daughter's bedroom. He closes his eyes and hears a gasping sound. He opens his eyes as a tear rolls down his face. He turns walks to his bedroom and slowly closes the door behind him.

THE NEXT MORNING

Peter is sitting by the kitchen table drinking his cup of coffee as he watches his daughter Natalie get on the school bus happily and excited because today is the last day of school. His eyes sadden and tire while watching the school bus drive away. Peter gets up from his chair and walks to the coat hanger. He puts on his jacket and walks out the door as he stands outside at the entrance of his house. He hears a rasping voice from within his mind say, ***"Sour isn't, to live in fear?"*** Peter closes his eyes slowly, the door behind him closes as he hears, ***"She's ours, and we will take her from you!"*** The voices end with a hysterical insane laughter. Peter's eyes open, he raises his eyes up to the hazy morning sky and walks down the steps to his car. Peter gets onto the New Jersey Parkway south bound towards a town called Newark. He sees that he is approaching traffic. He stops and waits as the State Police pass him by. He looks through his rear view mirror and sees the person inside the car behind him. The person's head begins to shake violently and suddenly pauses with a halt. Peter turns around to see the person in the car next to him. Her head is shaking too. All Peter could see in front of him were people's heads rattling inside their cars. Screams begin to come out from the cars around him. The screams grow louder and more frightening. Peter closes his eyes, covers his ears and yells out, ***"Oh God, Stop!"*** Then just like that the screams end. He opens his eyes. The honking of the cars behind him frazzle him. Peter then notices the car in front of him driving away. He turns to his right and notices the passenger looking directly at him like he was a jerk-off. The car drives away. He hears the passenger in back of him yelling, ***"Come on, move!"*** Peter drives away.

He finally arrives at Dr. Woods' office. He parks and goes into the office. He says to the receptionist, ***"Hi Judy."***

She replies, ***"Good morning Mr. Marks, Dr. Woods is expecting you. You can go right in."*** He knocks on the door and hears a voice from within say, ***"Come in."***

Peter goes in and says, ***"Hey Doc."*** Peter proceeds and closes the door behind him.

Dr. Woods says with a smile, ***"Hey Peter."***

Peter walks towards him and shakes his hand. He sits and Dr. Woods leans back on his chair shocked by Peter's appearance he says, ***"Jesus Peter, what happened to you? God you look like shit!"***

Peter says, ***"Well Dennis, my dreams are not getting any better, what do you expect from a man that hasn't slept?"***

Dr. Woods asks, ***"Still having those nightmares? I thought you told me a year ago that the dreams ended."***

Peter says to him, ***"They did, in a way, but these nightmares are not like the others I had. These dreams are worse!"***

Dr. Woods says to Peter, ***"Alright let me look at the notes, I have your file here."*** As Dr. Woods looks through Peter's record, Peter rests his arm upon the chair and holds his head. ***"Okay"***, Peter looks up.

Dr. Woods goes on to read, ***"We both know that you had insomnia, sometimes when you fell asleep you had disturbing dreams. It seems that they suddenly stopped with the medication I gave you and it has been***

a year since you've had a sleepless night, so I thought! You have been suffering from this disorder for a while, ever since, Debbie's death. I'm going to read to you some entries from the journal I've kept about your case. Let's see if we can come to some conclusion about why you are having these recurrent dreams!"

In 1993 you said that at night while sleeping you saw Debbie come to you, although you knew that it was impossible because she was dead. (Debbie was ill with cancer and had killed herself due to the depression and pain she was suffering.) Images of what Dr. Woods is saying come to Peter's mind.

One night a week later after the burial, you said that she appeared to you with others. Now these others that were with her, you said were demons! (In his mind Peter hears his wife calling him.) Dr. Woods looks up at Peter and goes on to say, ***"These demons began***

to beat your wife." (Peter begins to weep as the images in his mind echo with cynical laughter.) Dr. Woods pauses for a moment seeing that Peter is in distress. He asks him, ***"Do you want me to continue?"***

Peter with his hands on his head nods yes. Dr. Woods leans back in his chair. He takes off his glasses watching Peter weep in torment; he asks him, ***"Peter tell me about these new dreams that you've been having. As your friend and doctor I want and need to know why you are having these dreams. Hey, I just do not understand how when things seemed to get better for you, now all of a sudden you are having these dreams again! Why do you think they came back?"***

Peter with tears in his eyes replies, ***"They never went away! I was afraid that you might think I was self-destructive and that I might hurt Natalie or myself.***

I thought you might consider committing me into some nut house! What would become of Nat if that were to happen?"

Dr. Woods leans forward and says, *"Let me tell you something Peter, how could you ever think I would do something like that? We've known each other such a long time, don't you trust me? I know something like that would hurt you and Natalie! I would never jeopardize your lives."*

Peter looked up to him and said, *"I need your help, I'm falling apart!"*

Dr. Woods says, *"Peter you know all I want to do is to help you, tell me some more about what has been happening to you. If you want me to help you tell me everything."*

Peter begins to tell Dr. Woods about his nightmares, *"The dreams are far worse than you can*

imagine. You may not believe me or you might. You may come to a conclusion that I am crazy!"

Dr. Woods nodding no to what Peter is saying says to him, ***"Peter you know very well that I am the only person that can help you! There has to be a reason why all of these things are reoccurring."***

Peter looks up to Dr. Woods and says, ***"There has to be a logical explanation why I have been experiencing these dreams."***

Dr. Woods asks, ***"What do you mean?"***

Peter tells Dr. Woods, ***"I think that there is some dark evil oppressing me."***

Dr. Woods tells Peter, ***"There's no such thing. It's all in your mind. You are stressed out. You haven't been the same since Debbie's death. You're afraid of being alone which is perfectly normal. Since then, what***

your subconscious has done is created these <u>things</u> that are pursuing you."

Peter interrupts Dr. Woods saying, ***"I'm sorry Dennis, you're wrong this time. I have never been a church attendee. I am not a religious man, you know that, but I've come to a conclusion that yes, there is such a thing as evil."***

Peter leans forward on his chair, his eyes open wide and tear as he says softly. ***"I see them even when I am awake... I can hear them. They find pleasure watching me suffer. I pray like I have never prayed before. I pray that my daughter is safe."***

Dr. Woods asks Peter, ***"What's going on with Natalie? What does she have to do with your dreams?"***

Peter sits back and releases a low weep like a child. He nods yes. Peter goes onto recap. ***"One night I got up from my bed to check up on Natalie and***

as I approached her bedroom door I began to hear whispering voices coming from within." Peter pauses for a moment as Dr. Woods watches him. Peter lifts his eyes up to Dr. Woods saying, ***"As I opened the door slowly, the light of the hall lit the dark bedroom. Upon her bed were these dark human-like creatures, demons. They turned their heads and stared at me with cold white eyes."*** A howling cry came from them as Natalie sat up in her bed saying; (Peter extends his arms reaching out as if Natalie were there in front of him.) ***"Daddy help me don't let them take me!"*** Out of the darkness of the room on the floor were bodies twitching and moving around her bed. These bodies were wrapped in sheets. They sat up and began to scream, ***"Save her Peter, save her!"*** (Peter begins to sob as he speaks) ***"I look to Natalie and I see them***

grabbing and pulling her into the darkness behind her. Every night I have these dreams. They come to me and I don't know why. What do they want with her or what do they mean? Why me? What the fuck did I ever do to deserve this? I just want to know if I'm going insane or what?"

Dr. Woods looks down and says, *"Peter I'm going to speak with a doctor whom is a colleague of mine. I am going to consult this case with him and I'll find an answer to your questions. Your problem is far more obscure than I thought. I think Dr. Fisher can help us get to the bottom of this. I want you to take this medication called diazepam or more commonly called Valium. This medication is amongst a group of anti-anxiety drugs that will help you to reduce the experience of high anxiety in your life right now. This will enable you to relax. I don't want you to have a nervous*

breakdown. I will call you as soon as I speak to Dr. Fisher. Is that all right with you?" Dr. Woods hand Peter his prescription and says, ***"I'll call you. You can call me anytime day or night. It doesn't matter!"***

Peter looks up to Dr. Woods and says, ***"Thank you."*** They both stand up from their chairs and shake hands. Dr. Woods says to Peter, ***"Don't forget, call me if you need me."***

Peter smiles and says, ***"I will, thank you again Dennis."*** Dr. Woods walks across the office with Peter and opens the door for him. Peter pats Dr. Woods on his shoulder, smiles and walks out.

Wednesday

Late that Night

Peter lies on the sofa with Natalie asleep by his side. He slowly opens his eyes and stretches. He looks at the clock up on the wall. He notices it's one o'clock in the morning. He gently picks her up and takes her upstairs to her bedroom. He opens the bedroom door quietly, walks over to her bed and lays her down on it. He tucks Natalie in. He hears a heavy asthmatic breathing sound in the room. He covers his daughter and stands up. He turns walks to the light switch to turn the lights on but they do not turn on. Peter hears a voice speak out to him, a rasping voice that says, ***"What would a father do to save his child."*** Peter looks across the dark room trying to see where the voice is coming from. He speaks out to it, ***"Show yourself Goddamn it!"*** Peter quickly turns the light switch on and off. The lights turned on. He looks across the bedroom. He does not see anything. Peter turns to Natalie and sees that she is sound asleep. He turns the light off and grabs a rocking chair that is by her bed. He sits next to her. He then closes his eyes.

Morning Came

The bedroom lights up with the brightness of the sun. Natalie wakes up, she turns and notices her father sitting beside her asleep. She gets up and says to him, ***"Dad."*** Peter opens his eyes and sees Natalie looking at him with a gentle smile, he smiles back.

Natalie says to her father, ***"Bad dreams?"***

He sits up and stretches saying, ***"You want to know the truth? No, I did not have any bad dreams."***

"That's good." Says Natalie.

Peter says to her, ***"You know what? Tomorrow we are going to Adventure Park."***

She quickly gets out of bed and hugs him saying, ***"I love you Daddy."***

"I love you too baby. Go and shower, I want us to have a fun day today. I want to take you to the mall and buy you what you wanted for your birthday. Call some of your friends we'll all go."

"All right!" Says Natalie as she walks out the room.

Peter lies back on the chair looking across the room. He closes his eyes.

At the mall, Natalie and her friends walk in front of Peter. Laughing and talking they run towards a store window that Natalie sees and she turns to her father saying, ***"Dad look at these cool boots!"*** Peter slowly walks smiling towards them as he turns towards a crowd of people whom are walking towards him. He stops and within the crowd he sees dark human-form shadows approaching. Their heads start to rattle violently. Peter slowly turns to his daughter as she is talking to her friends. She looks back at him and silence fills his ears. Peter turns towards the crowd. The shadows slowly transform into ghoulish creatures without any facial features. It's almost as if the skin of their faces were stretched and pulled back. As Natalie and her friends walk into the store, her friends slowly turn to Natalie with wicked smiles! Their eyes roll white. Natalie turns to her father frightened.

She yells, ***"Dad!"***

Her voice echoes in his head. Peter is paralyzed. He wants to run to her but he can't move. He watches as Natalie's friends shove her to the floor. His heart pounds heavily with fear. Peter looks into his daughter's eyes as they begin to tear blood.

She cries out to him, ***"Save me daddy!"***

A rusty chain wraps itself around her neck. It drags her body towards the crowd of people that change into demonic ghouls. These bodies turn and lift her lifeless body over them pulling her down into the crowd. Peter's ears fill with tormenting screams. He is still unable to move! He wants to scream but no sound comes out of his mouth. He can only close his eyes. He hears a voice calling to him saying, ***"Dad, Dad!"***

Peter opens his eyes and turns to the voice, it was Natalie. As the crowd walks past him he walks towards her and she asks him, ***"Dad are you okay? You were spaced out!"*** Peter's eyes roll back and he passes out. His head hits the floor. Peter regains consciousness and notices that he is on a stretcher. Around him are a doctor and nurse pushing the stretcher down a long endless bright hall. Peter looks up and asks the doctor, ***"Doctor where am I?"*** As Peter's eyes wonder, the hall lights blind him each time they pass over him. He looks up towards the doctor that is behind him. Peter begins to scream! The doctor's head starts rattling then stops! The skin on his face is pulled back as he smiles at Peter and says, ***"Peter, Peter it's just the beginning!"***

Peter wakes up

He turns over on his side and sees Natalie and Dr. Woods. Dr. Woods tells Peter, ***"Jesus Peter, you gave us quite a scare!"***

Peter asks, ***"What happened to me, where am I?"*** Out of breath he looks around the room. Dr. Woods settles him down and says, ***"Relax! You passed out at the mall when you were with Natalie!"***

Natalie holds her father's hand.

Dr. Woods tells Peter, ***"Peter I told you, you have to take it easy! Do you know that you could of had a heart attack? You're going to stay here for a couple of days to have some tests run to see if everything is alright."***

Confused, Peter puts his hands on his head and asks, ***"How long have I been here?"***

"Two days, you've been unconscious!" Says Dr. Woods.

Peter looks at Natalie and feels terrible for what happened on her birthday. He says to her, ***"I'm so sorry baby!"***

"For what Dad?"

"For messing up your birthday!"

"Ooh Dad, don't worry, I just want you to be ok!"

Dr. Woods turns to Peter saying, ***"Listen I'll see you tomorrow. You relax ok! I'll take Natalie to her grandmother's house. You take care of yourself and I'll see you later."*** They shake hands.

Peter says, ***"Fine Doc."*** He kisses and hugs Natalie goodbye saying, ***"Listen Natalie, if you need me call me or Dr. Woods alright?"*** She nods yes. ***"I love you, bye baby!"*** He says as he kisses her again. He takes a deep breath and closes his eyes. As they walk out of the room the on call doctor walks in. The room darkens....

Late into the night

In Dr. Woods's study at his house, he sits behind his desk speaking into a recorder,keeping file of Peter's latest incidents and progress each time they've met.

"Everyday and every night Peter's life gets darker and complex into a realm of insanity. His nights become a feast of tears. Fears become terror, as his nightmares are no longer just dreams! He says demons possess his mind. Tormenting his life. Dr. Fisher, a colleague of mine who is specialized in Peter's condition is helping me treat Peter. We ponder into Peter's disorder. Dr. Fisher came to a conclusion that Peter suffers from an illness called <u>sleep terror disorder</u>. A disorder that is characterized by recurrent episodes of waking up in what seems to be a state of extreme anxiety. When the patient wakes he/she experiences rapid breathing and accelerated pulse. Once

the individual settles down he/she usually recalls a vague sense of terror.

Dr. Woods recollects Peter's encounters not only as nightmares but also when he is awake.

We have also summed-up Peter's condition not only as sleep terror disorder but also another illness called paranoia delusional disorder. Each day I see a dear friends life burn before my eyes due to these supposed illnesses. A man who had a life that was sweet but became sour. In reality I don't know why all this is happening to him but Peter is slowly loosing it all!

Six months later

Dr. Woods and Dr. Fisher are having lunch; they are discussing several cases they are working on together. They come upon the topic of Peter.

They agree that they need to moderate his medication and monitor his progress.

Dr. Woods tells Dr. Fisher, ***"Peter has slowly realized that all these experiences have all been in his mind."***

Dr. Fisher takes a sip of his wine and says, ***"Yes, let's monitor his medications to see if there are any changes in his behavior!"***

"It's only normal he would go into such depression. Anyone would if they had witnessed the suicide of their loved one!" Adds Dr. Woods. He goes onto say, ***"According to Peter he has not had anymore disturbing dreams. This doesn't mean that he's cured but it's a good sign and a step ahead to find clues about his illness!***

Peter walks into Dr. Woods' office several weeks later

Dr. Woods and Dr. Fisher are talking about a golf tournament that their local club is hosting. Surprised to see Peter, Dr. Woods and Dr. Fisher say, ***"Hello Peter, how are you?"***

"Good morning Dr. Woods and Dr. Fisher."

Dr. Woods looks at Peter and asks, ***"What brings you here? You're appointment isn't until next week! Are you alright?"***

Peter smiles doubtfully and says, ***"Oh yeah, I'm fine, since I was in the area I came to get another appointment card from Janet for the appointment because I misplaced the original one."***

Dr. Woods says, ***"Sure I'll ask Janet to make you out another card, but Peter you could have called! Are you sure you're okay?"***

Peter looks down for a moment and says, ***"Yes, I'm fine, I'll see you next week. I'm going to spend some quality time with my daughter today, especially after all the things that have happened. In the past year and a half she hasn't had any normalcy in her life and it's not fair to her. She's only a child!"***

Dr. Fisher says, ***"That's great, you should spend some quality time with her!"***

Meanwhile, Dr. Woods excuses himself as he goes out to get another appointment card from Janet.

Dr. Fisher continues on to say, ***"Spending time with each other will help your relationship with her but also help to distract your mind. So where are you going to take her?"***

Peter tells him, ***"I'm going to take her to the Adventure Park. She's wanted to go there for a really***

long time. There is a new roller coaster that she wants us to ride! I just hope that I can keep up with her!" Dr. Fisher laughs along with Peter.

Dr. Woods walks back into the office and hands Peter the appointment card and says, ***"Here you are Peter, I overheard you say your going to take Natalie to Adventure Park, have a great time! We'll talk about your day with her on your next visit, all right? So go and enjoy yourself."***

Peter smiles and says, ***"Definitely, thank you!"***

Dr. Woods smiling walks Peter to the door and watches him go down the hall. Dr. Woods turns to Dr. Fisher who is standing by the desk and says, ***"I hope that man can find peace in his mind!"*** Dr. Woods slowly closes the door behind him.

It was a sunny afternoon

Peter takes Natalie to Adventure Park where he promised her he would take her on her 12th birthday almost two years ago. As they walk talking and laughing they enjoy themselves. The park is filled with people. Peter points to a bench. They walk across the crowd and sit together facing the park's pond. At the pond there are a couple of ducks swimming in the sun. Peter stares at the ducks as they swim in front of them quacking away at each other. Natalie sits looking at her father's face. She has a funny feeling that this is the last time she'll see him. She asks him, "***Dad, what's wrong?***"

Peter turns and looks at her, then back and forth to her and the ground. He looks up to her and says, ***"You know that I love you right?"***

He holds her hand and continues to say, ***"I just want to say I'm so sorry for not being the father that every other kid has. I know all the things that have been going on seem weird and I'm sorry for leaving you by yourself with Grandma. In these last two years I've seen you grow into an independent young lady. You took care of me when I needed you and I thank you for that. I couldn't have asked for a better daughter. You never questioned why, you where just there for me!"***

As Natalie listens to her father she looks up to him and says, ***"Dad you don't have to say you're sorry, I know you love me. I always felt your love, even through the pain you have suffered. You showed how much you loved me in your own nutty way!"*** They smile and Peter says to her, ***"Listen, the past is the***

past. From today on, you and I will make it! I know Mom would have wanted it that way."

Natalie reaches over to him, they hug and Peter says, ***"I love you baby."***

Natalie hears people screaming and yelling. She turns to see the main attraction, the roller coaster called, ***"Diablo," one of the fastest and bad rides ever built.***

"Dad come on let's ride that one! I want to ride it with you. Cindy told me that she rode it with her kid brother and it made him barf! Come on Dad!" She grabs her father by the arm and pulls him off the bench.

"Great", says Peter unexcited. ***"A ride that makes people throw up. Oh yeah, that's my type of ride!"***

"Come on", says Natalie laughing and running through the crowd around the pond. They finally reach the line of the ride. Peter looks up and notices a sign over their heads that reads, ***An hour wait for the new cliff-hanging, heart-stopping, spine-tingling ride, Diablo. "Oh man this is going to be good!"*** Says Natalie excited and filled with anticipation. Peter breathes in and out as the hot sun beats down on them. He looks down at his daughter that is so excited to be there with him. He smiles putting his hand on her head. Slowly the line begins to move. Peter hears a heavy gasp behind him. He turns around and sees a teenage boy who is asthmatic. The boy reaches into his pocket for his inhaler. Peter laughs with relief! Natalie looks up at him smiling. She asks him, ***"Nervous? Just to let you know Dad, this ride has four big drops, six loops and is extremely fast!"***

Peter says, ***"Nervous? Yes! You know I was looking at that nice gentle baby dragon kiddy ride over there."*** He smiles at Natalie who is looking up at him and says smiling at her, ***"It's just been a long time since I've been on one of these things."***

Above them the roller coaster roars by as Natalie is thrilled by the excited screams of the people. Peter and Natalie walk up the steps. They are the next group up! ***Diablo*** *is the 20 cart long serpent, red and black with a huge head of the Devil as the front cart. It's eyes are painted black and it has a long green tongue.* Over Peter's head are huge speakers with hellish sound effects of a tremendous roar. Sounds of an angry beast and a monstrous voice laughs and says, ***"Welcome to your nightmare!"***

Peter watches as the roller coaster takes off into the dark tunnel followed by another coaster. Natalie looks up to him and asks smiling, ***"Ready Dad?"*** Peter claps his hands and says, ***"Most definitely!"*** The roller coaster stops and the safety bars rise up. The passengers stand up to step out of the ride and the new passengers step in. Peter and Natalie sit in the ride, Natalie excited says, ***"Ooh man, this is going to be so cool!"*** She reaches into her jean jacket pocket and pulls out a piece of gum. She pops it into her mouth as the attendants walk up and down the aisle making sure that the safety bars are locked and secured. At the far end a voice yells out, ***"Good to go!"*** The ride begins to move as the people start to scream and cheer as the roller coaster rides into the dark tunnel.

Peter screams out to Natalie, ***"You never told me this ride was in the dark!"*** Natalie cheers out loud. The roller coaster begins to climb, Peter squints due to the bright strobe lights. Just when it reaches the top, before the deep drop into what looks like an endless abyss, a tremendous roaring voice says, ***"I am Diablo!"*** Then suddenly it drops and Peter closes his eyes as he hears the people screaming. He feels something tapping his hand! It's Natalie! Peter turns his head and notices by the flickering lights· that Natalie is choking! She leans forward when suddenly her head is whipped back by the force of the ride. 'Peter panics.' He can't move due to the safety bars holding him back. The roller coaster finally goes outside. As it climbs for another drop Natalie's lips turn blue! Peter screams frantically, ***"Oh my God!"*** as he panics! He turns and looks forward to the front of the ride all the heads of the passenger's turn completely towards them. Their heads begin to rattle! The ride reaches the top and drops. Peter feels Natalie's hand squeezing his. He cries out as the roller coaster hits the last drop before ending. The passengers yell out, ***"Save her Peter, save her!"*** Laughter fills his ears. Peter screams out, ***"Take me, please let my daughter go, goddamn you!"*** Voices come out from their blurry rattling heads, they speak out at the same time, ***"Seeing you live in suffering is such pleasure. What would you give up? What would you do to save her?"***

Peter filled with rage screams out with all his might, ***"Take me. I give up my soul to you!"***

The roller coaster drops, rides up a loop and goes down a long track slowly reaching its destination. The passengers on the ride yell laughing with excitement as the ride comes to an end. The next crowd of passengers wait eagerly for their turn. A woman screams out, ***"Oh my God!"*** She points as the ride attendant's rush towards Peter's lifeless body leaning forward. Natalie holds her father's hand crying out, ***"Daddy, Dad. Daddy!"*** One of the ride attendants yells out, ***"Hurry! Call 911!"*** They lift Peter's head up, his face is pale and he has a painful expression on his face. With help, Natalie steps out of the cart and the attendants hold her trying to calm her down. She cries out, ***"Dad, Dad!!"***

In a dark tormenting place filled with lamenting screams Peter is dangling wrapped in chains drenched in blood. Voices scream out his daughter's name, "Natalie!"

"What would you do to save your own?"

I learned never to speak about yesterday. The day of black, the past is something that I dread to remember. Fear is dormant for now. The things that torment me wait patiently in the dark corners of my mind. My eyes are scared by the images they glance upon. Images of what lurks in my life, surround me with misery taking away piece by piece my life. All I have is a prayer. I pray and pray that tomorrow I may smile with hope. Oh, what an uncertain future without meaning, with a smile I hide my demons and hope I'll find peace tomorrow...

A young woman sitting in a library slowly turns towards a gasping voice calling out to her, *"Susan."*

Do you ever wonder if your life is a dream? For some, life is a dream filled with pleasures beyond belief. There are people that do not want to go to sleep fearing that if they do, their sweet dreams could all come to an end. Life can be so good, a blessing when everything looks like a dream. Yet, for others, day after day their life is not a sweet dream but a nightmare. These people suffer such pain beyond comprehension that they would give anything to go to sleep and wake in peace. In their lives there is no tranquility, there are no sweet dreams. Their lives are oppressed by darkness. The only words that roll out from their lips are, ***"Oh God, when will this end?"*** As I look up to the sky, the hope within me slowly dies, my eyes swell with tears and I feel alone in this world.

I went to the great city to the tallest tower that had ever been built. I went in and climbed to the top. When I finally reached the top I walked out into the open, slowly I approached the edge, my eyes opened with amazement to see myself on top of the world. Across the horizon, the great city lied beneath my feet. The sight was breathtaking. I lifted my head to the heavens and closed my eyes, the wind blew its cool breath against my face and the sun shined its warmth upon me. The sense of hope began to grow within me once again.

Suddenly, there was a frightening loud scream echoing across the city. I opened my eyes and looked down towards the city. An unpleasant feeling came over me as I looked down below. I noticed creeping within the building a black thick fog. It was like a shadow coming towards the tower.

The wind grew cold. I looked around towards the sky and noticed the sun's light slowly dimming. Finally dying out until I felt the brutal cold winds. Fear began to posses me. A dark black fog was approaching. I began to hear cries within the fog as it drew closer and closer. As the painful cries faded I stepped back as the fog crept up the tower from down below. I heard weeping then screams mixed with laughter. I watched the creeping black vapor slowly climb over the edge as it flowed towards me. I saw within the fog, images of things that I have seen in my sleep. Things that feed upon the fears of man turning him into a slave of his own fears. I have seen these dark demonic creatures come to me in my mind. When I sleep these dark angels wake to feast on my sanity. A black tall human form shadow walked out of the black mist and stood before me. It had no facial form. It was growling with anger and called my name, ***"Michael.."*** In a whispering angry tone Michael replied frightened by what stood before him, ***"What do you want with me?"*** It's head started to rattle viciously as it said, ***"I came from the regions of your deepest darkest desires. There is a place for you here. A place where fields of lost prayers linger in time. Where lost souls beg to be found. A place of pain and misery, a place beyond torment. A place where you will suffer tears of blood. You belong to me and Hell awaits your endless suffering."*** Within the fog were mumbled whispers. Michael confused said, ***"I don't understand, what did I do?"*** Michael suddenly grew ill, he fell to his knees. Crouched forward in pain he lifted his head and looked to his left. He saw his lifeless body on the floor. Flashing in his mind was an image of a young woman opening a cellar door, calling out his name, ***"Michael, Michael",*** she walked down the stairs. As she reached for the light and turned it on she saw the grim sight of Michael's lifeless body hanging from his neck! She walked towards him in disbelief as her eyes swelled with tears. She noticed a letter tightly clenched in his hand. She tried to pry it out without tearing it. She finally removed it and began to read it. It read, ***"Forgive me for what I have done, but I can't bear this anymore! I hope in death I can find peace because in life all I had was misery!"*** The young woman wept as she looked up to his body that was gently swinging side to side. Her eyes noticed shadows behind his body in the darkness of the cellar coming towards her! Suddenly, the cellar door slammed shut and the light died out. Within the darkness there was a weeping moan. Michael lifted his head and saw a dark figure standing before him. It said, ***"It's time!"*** Out of the mist, demons approached him. Their heads began to jar as they reached out for him. Quickly, Michael turned to run he bumped into the young woman. A chain wrapped around Michael's neck cutting him. The woman's face was pale like death. She leaned over to him. Her eyes were open. They looked like two empty black pits staring straight at him. She smiled, Michael screamed. The chains yanked him to the ground dragging his body like a piece of meat. Before falling over the edge, he sees himself being dragged across a garden. His eyes open wide in shock as he passes by a statue. (His body continues to be dragged throughout the garden). He holds onto the chain. He hears screaming all around him as his body is violently pulled through the garden. The chains around his neck unwrap and drag away into the darkness of the mist. Michael's body tumbled and ended up in a pothole filled with mud. Laughter mixed with painful cries fills the air.

As time slipped by he awoke by a chilling frightening howl. His eyes opened, they wandered slowly with pain. As he sat up he heard a sound of dangling chains like the sound of a rusty swing behind him. Slowly he turned to look back and from a distance hanging by chains is what appeared to be a person in a wheelchair. Michael got up on his feet and slowly walked towards the image dangling a few yards from him. As Michael got closer and closer he noticed that the body was hanging by hooks! The body gently swung side to side. Its head leaned to one side. Michael is underneath this poor soul looking up to it as it hung from a tree branch.

Michael stared into the face. The young man in the wheelchair was Jacob! His face reflected pain. A voice behind him said, ***"Hey you!"*** He turned to see a man sitting on the ground strapped in a straight jacket. His face was pale and his eyes were rolled back into his head, he said to Michael along with the many sounds and voices speaking all at once, ***"Peace to those who suffer in their own Hell."*** There were gasping sounds surrounding Michael as he began to hear a chorus of anguished cries saying, ***"This is Hell my friend. Don't let its beauty deceive you!"*** The man lifted his head up to the sky and screamed out, ***"Oh God save me, save me from this place!"***

Michael turned back and saw from the ground, rising with screams, dark shadows slowly twisting into form. Michael looked down to the man in the straight jacket overwhelmed with fear. He turned and ran away from the shadows. He had no idea where he was going. As he was running away the shadows took their form. Their heads jolted like the tail of a rattlesnake. They looked to the man and walked towards him. Behind him, Michael heard a painful wail but he did not look back. He tried to get as far away as possible. The garden slowly began to grow dark. As the sounds in the air intensified with frightening screams, the torture grew with anguish. There was a chorus of suffering cries beyond any that the human ear has ever heard. Michael out of breath stopped running and came to rest upon a tree. He leaned against it trying to catch his breath. He looked back to see the lonely garden filled with statues. Silence surrounded him. It was as if he had grown deaf all of a sudden. He looked around as he walked. He noticed in the distance a fog slowly creeping towards him. He looked behind and saw nothing, just the garden. He looked forward. The thick dark fog drew closer. Coming out of the ground he saw souls buried up to their necks. Their heads stuck out of the ground as if they were in tombs. Michael began to back away from them as he heard their moans and cries. He stopped and covered his ears. He fell to his knees.

Suddenly, arms came out of the ground reaching out for their heads as these grotesque demonic ghouls fed upon them sinking them back into the earth. It was the most frightening sound Michael had ever heard. The poor souls screamed out to him. He saw the pain, the suffering in their eyes as their tears slowly rolled down their faces until he could only hear their cries underneath the ground.

The fog took its path towards Michael. His mind ached. Michael began to feel all over him the long dull suffering of those who were being fed upon. The pain he felt was unbearable!

Michael fell to the ground. The smog surrounded him. He saw himself within the fog. His eyes filled with tears. His face reflected the stress that he felt inside. He heard gasping voices all around, calling out his name. Within the voices he heard laughter and multiple voices repeating over and over in a rasping tone, ***"Sinner, Sinner, Sinner."*** He saw in the mist black images moving rapidly crisscrossing each other approaching him. Michael looked up to the sky. His eyes swelled. He saw the dying light of the sun slowly fading to black. The air grew with a fowl stench of death. Michael began to feel repulsed. He cried, ***"Father who are in Heaven***

save me!" A monstrous voice said, ***"Never, Never. God can't hear you here!"*** Michael saw within the fog harp shaped gates slowly opening. He crawled to get up and blindly ran through the fog towards the gates. Behind him he heard the shadows approach saying, ***"Run, run all you can, you will not get away!"*** He reached the gates and passed them without noticing that he was running into the thick fog. As the two fogs merged together it drifted to the other side of the gates. Slowly the gates closed with hellish screams.

Time passed by

The gates slowly opened and behind it the thick fog from outside lingered. Within the fog Michael saw an image approach him slowly, it became clearer and clearer as it got closer, it was an image of a woman's body wrapped in wet white sheets pressed against her body. Her arms reached out in front of her as she floated over the ground towards Michael. She stopped at the entrance of the dark harped shaped gates. The fog began to dissolve with piercing hellish screeches. Within it Michael could see the fires of Hell. Burning in the flames were demons feasting upon those who suffered in it. He could see impaled bodies rotting in the air. Men and women, young and old, suffered unspeakable torture. He felt the hot winds of Hell against his face. The demonic ghouls tortured by inflicting pain beyond belief. Demons bathed in blood as a chorus of tormented cries. Sounds beyond any sound that haunts the human mind. He directed his eyes beyond the gates and saw ruined souls reach out begging for mercy.

Chains wrapped around his waist held his body. His head began to jolt out of control. As he cried, demons tormented him. From below one of them jumped up and took hold of his legs, as it climbed up his body. The gates began to close. The fog took form again until consuming the horror that lied within its midst. You heard the sound of a loon echoing throughout the mist. Chills run up your spine knowing that the world is too naïve to realize that

Hell Awaits...

A young man is suddenly awakened from his sleep terrified. He sits up in his bed soaked in sweat, breathing heavily and staring straight ahead. His wife worried, tries to calm him calling out his name, ***"Glenn…"***

It is cold and gray. The winds of December blow its harsh breath down upon a young woman walking across a college campus. She walks towards a church. Her eyes are swollen with tears. Her face reflects exhaustion. Trembling, she looks both ways before crossing the street. She crosses carefully. Susan comes to the steps of a church and pauses. Slowly she lifts up her head. The doors of the church burst open with an angry growl. She closes her eyes. She feels something unpleasant approaching her from behind. In a rasping voice whispers in her ears say, ***"Peace you seek, peace you will not find!"*** The young woman sobs. ***"Susan",*** she hears someone call her. She turns towards the voice and sees a statue of St. Anthony looking down at her. It turns its head and smiles. She turns and runs away down the street towards the dorms. Susan runs into her dorm room shaking and crying. She slams the door shut. Laughter fills her ears and the voices in her head say, ***"We are back and this time we are going to take you, not even your mother's prayers will save you!"*** She cries out in anguish. She runs to her phone picks it up and begins to dial. On the other end of the line, the phone begins to ring. A voice answers, ***"Hello?"***

"Mom it's me, Susan."

"Susan?"

"Mommy, they're back!"

"Who? What are you talking about? Who is back?"

"Them, Mom, them!!"

The phone goes dead! ***"Mother? Mom?"*** Susan cries and desperately throws the phone down. She runs out the room down the hall out the dorm building towards her car. She gets in and drives off frantically. Susan drives down the street and hops onto the Garden State Parkway northbound. Her mind is tormented with laughter. She turns on the radio puts the volume up loud to drown out the voices that taunt her. As she drives down the parkway she looks through her rearview mirror, she sees Christ and the Devil in the back seat laughing together at her! She weeps, ***"Leave me alone!"*** The Devil mocks her cries saying, ***"Leaving me alone!"*** Christ laughs!

Susan shakes her head and drives on. After two hours or so of driving she gets off onto a small country town road and drives down the lonely dusty path. At the end of the road up on a small hill stands a house with dark woods surrounding it. Susan's eyes tear when her eyes catch sight of her parent's house. She drives around the bend and up to the front. Susan knocks at the front door. The knocks echo throughout the inner walls of the house. Susan hears her mother say, ***"I'm coming",*** as she walks towards the door. She opens the door and says, ***"Susan!"*** Susan looks up, her eyes roll back as she says in a gasping voice, ***"Mom".*** She faints, dropping into her mother's arms. Her mother screams out, ***"Lewis help me, it's Susan!"***

Time passes by

Susan awakens sweating and shaking, her eyes wonder lost, and she slowly sits up in her bed. She calls out for her mother. The bedroom door slowly opens and her mother walks in saying, ***"Honey?"*** Susan reaches out to her with her arms extended, her eyes roll back while crying she says, ***"Pray for me!"*** She screams! Her body begins to shake violently and she passes out! Her face has a pale death-like appearance. Her mother runs out of the room calling out to Susan's father. From downstairs her father rushes to meet his wife who is trembling and crying. She says, ***"It's happening again!"***

"What?' He asks, ***"What?"*** Her father walks into the frigid room. He sees his daughter speaking in another language with her eyes closed. Susan turns her head towards him and smiles. Her father turns and walks out of the room closing the door behind him. He holds his wife saying, ***"This can't happen, not again!"*** He looks at his wife who is sobbing in his arms.

Susan's father walks towards the steps and turns to Susan's mother saying, ***"Keep and eye on her."*** She looks at the bedroom door and behind it, she hears laughter. Susan's father walks down the stairs to the phone. He looks up St. Paul's Church in the directory, and dials the number. A woman answers the phone and says, ***"St. Paul's, how may I help you?"***

"Yes hello, who am I speaking to?"

"Martha Temple"

"Hello Ms. Temple. Is Father James there? I need to speak to him urgently. It is very important! Please!"

"May I ask who is calling?"

"This is Mr. Martin!"

"Alright Mr. Martin I'm going to transfer you, please hold."

Father James, a middle aged, tall, slender man with glasses is sitting in his room at his desk reading. His phone rings, he walks over and answers, ***"Hello?"***

Hysterically, Mr. Martin calls out, ***"Father James this is Mr. Martin"***

"Yes Mr. Martin how are you?"

"Father James are you busy right now? There is something going on in my house that I really need you to see. It's happening again to Susan…"

Father James confused asks, ***"What? Calm down! What are you talking about? What is happening again?"***

After hearing Mr. Martin's description of Susan's condition, his face froze. You can hear Mr. Martin on the phone pleading, ***"Please Father you***

have to come to my house! Oh God, how can this happen again? I just don't understand how!"

Later that evening

The doorbell rings, Mr. Martin opens the door. Upstairs in her bedroom Susan's eyes open. Her eyes are lifeless as her head turns to the bedroom door.

"Hello Father James!"

Mr. Martin welcomes him in. As he steps into the house, a scream comes from upstairs. Everyone looks up. Mrs. Martin closes her eyes and begins to pray. Father James takes his hat off and turns to Mr. Martin asking, ***"Is she upstairs in her room?" Don't close the door Father O'Leary is coming, I told him***

what happened to Susan five years ago. He wants to see her also.

Father O'Leary walks in. He is an older man, shorter than Father James with hair streaked with gray. He says, ***"Hello, I'm Father O'Leary"***

"Come in Father."

Says Mr. Martin as he closes the door behind him. They all walk into the living room.

"I just don't understand how this could happen again!" Says Mrs. Martin. Father James turns to Mrs. Martin, ***"Take us to her."*** Mrs. Martin trembles as she leads them upstairs. As they walk up the stairs, they feel something pass them by. They hear screams as they make their way towards her bedroom. The house grows silent. Mr. Martin reaches for the doorknob. The bedroom door slowly opens and the two priests stand at the entrance of

Susan's room. Their eyes open wide gazing at the frightful sight of the young woman. She was sitting on the bed staring back at them. Her eyes were white and empty as she breathed laboriously through her mouth as if she were suffering from asthma. In their hearts, they are positive that this girl is possessed. The way it manifested itself. Out of Susan's mouth came the voices, ***"Are you here to save her from us?'***

"Susan, its Father James, remember me?"

She smiles her body tenses with anger. With a gasping voice she answers, ***"Come in Father we all know who you and your assistant are, step into darkness!"***

Father James and Father O'Leary walk into the room towards her. Susan stares them down. Her face is emotionless and pale. Father O'Leary sets his handbag on her dresser and looks up towards the mirror in front of him. Through the mirror he can see her ghoulish image staring back at him as they prepare.

"Why prepare? This time you will loose. Father James, this battle is lost!" Father O'Leary walks up to the bed, in his hand is the Bible. He opens it and begins to pray, reciting from Psalm 23: The Lord is my Shepherd I shalt not want..." After this he begins to pray, ***"Our Father whom art in Heaven..."***

Susan looks up at Father O'Leary saying, ***"I have my own prayers"***

She begins to speak in a strange language. Father James joins Father O'Leary in the prayer. Behind their voices they hear unnatural human cries. Father James does the sign of the cross in front of her. ***"In the name of the Lord Jesus Christ, I cast you out unclean spirit!"***

Father O'Leary blesses Susan with the Holy Water. When the drops fall upon her skin, her body jerks violently and she falls back onto the bed with her eyes closed. They begin to cast out the demons in Susan. Downstairs in the living room, Susan's parents are praying. Mrs. Martin looks up to the ceiling and the old chandelier's lights begins to flicker. The chandelier begins to swing side to side. They can hear Susan's painful cries.

Then there was silence

Mr. Martin stands and Mrs. Martin turns to him. Tears roll down her face. The chandelier slowly stops swinging. From the upstairs bedroom, the door violently swings open. The Martins hear footsteps running out from Susan's room down the hall and quickly down the stairs. The front door suddenly opens and leaves come tumbling in. Standing looking over the banister is Father James with Father O'Leary. Their faces drip with perspiration. Father O'Leary turns and walks back into Susan's room. Slowly he walks over to her, watching tears flow down her face as her eyes are closed. Susan is standing at the front door entrance trembling looking back at her parents but they cannot see her. Father James walks back into the bedroom. Quickly, Mr. Martin runs upstairs followed by Mrs. Martin. When they reach Susan's bedroom, they stand shocked at the entrance by what their eyes see. Mr. Martin nods no, in disbelief of what he sees, he cries out, ***"No God, no. Susan!"***

In anguish, he watches Father James try to resuscitate Susan. Her lips are blue. Her face is lifeless. Father James continues to give her CPR. Mrs. Martin stands crying by the door. Father O'Leary turns to her and runs towards Mrs. Martin grabbing her yelling, ***"Call 911!"*** She turns to him frozen in shock. Father O'Leary quickly walks out of the bedroom. Susan notices something slowly stepping out of her bedroom a tall black figure, its head bobbing faster and faster with every step it takes towards the stairs. Then its head began to rattle. Susan frightened turns to run out of the house. She is paralyzed with fear. Her eyes open wide by what she sees. Father O'Leary runs down the stairs into the living room. As he reaches for the telephone he hears a gasping whispering voice say, ***"Satanas".*** Father O'Leary turns around. He begins to feel an unpleasant presence in the living room, which is coming from within the darkness of the small passageway leading towards the kitchen. Father O'Leary opens his eyes and looks around. From upstairs Father James yells out to him, ***"Did you call 911?"*** He quickly turns to the telephone picks it up and notices his hand trembling. He dials 911. He holds his shaking hand. On the line a voice answers, ***"911, what is your emergency?"*** Father O'Leary hears a tapping sound. He looks up. Leaves come dancing in from the wind outside. The tapping sound of the doorknob gently hits the wall behind him. The tap echoes throughout the living room. The fog within the woods spill out into the moonlight. Within the thick mist, Susan can see dark figures walking towards her. Their faces have no facial features. Behind her, Susan hears the thing from her room creeping up behind her. She runs towards her car. When she reaches for the car door handle she can't grab hold of it. Suddenly, she hears, ***"Susan!"*** Her mother's voice. Susan looks up and sees her mother standing at the entrance of the house. Susan looks back, there is nothing there, no fog. There is just silence of the woods and darkness all around her. She turns back to her mother, ***"Mom!"***

Her mother begins to sing in multiple voices, *Ave Maria.* Blood begins to drip from her eyes, Susan screams hysterically. She hears laughter all around her mocking her suffering. She gazes at a twisted tree standing next to the house. Susan sees six bodies hanging from the branches. The bodies are bound by barbwire around their wrists and ankles. Blood drips from their tortured bodies. Their heads are covered with black hoods. Within their hoods, their heads rattle. Susan hears them cry in pain. Deep in the woods, Susan sees shadows moving towards her whispering her name, ***"Susan".*** Not knowing where to run she runs down the dirt road blinded by fear. She sees herself running into the woods like a scared rabbit being chased by wolves. They pursue her, tormenting her, ***"Run Susan, run!"*** Laughter mixes with screams, the shadows rapidly approach her. The dark woods fill with cries. Susan notices tall gates straight ahead. Thinking it might be someone's house she runs with all her might. Knowing that they are right behind her and approaching quickly, she passes the gates. Her ears are deaf with silence. Intimidated to look back, she realizes the silence. She turns to see and there is nothing, just the gates fading slowly into the darkness. She stops running. Out of breath, she falls to her knees. She looks up confused. She notices around her are beautiful statues of angels looking down on her. A statue of a woman weeping catches her eyes. Susan slowly stands up. She cannot believe what she is seeing. The place that she finds herself in is so beautiful and tranquil. Suddenly, leaves gently began to fall around her as if it were autumn. All different colors, red, yellow and purple. They cover the ground. Susan is amazed. She looks behind the trees, scattered all throughout the garden are statues. She walks up to one. It seems to be a man. Susan looks at its face and it is faded by time, as if it has stood there forever. It looks like the man is in anguish. Susan slowly reaches for it to touch its face. With her fingertips she feels the statue and withdraws her hand. She looks back at the statue and she feels its sorrow.

Susan turns and notices a lake behind the trees. She slowly walks towards it. A cool breeze blows on her face. She looks over the lake and across its dark motionless waters. Across from it, on the other side is a country view of green hills as far as the eye can see. Susan closes her eyes, takes a deep breath and feels a warm gentle wind caressing her body. Susan opens her eyes and she gazes upon a dark fog-like mist growing between the trees, which begins to flow down from the hills. It creeps towards the lake. She notices that everything in its path dies. Suddenly, the gentle warm wind turns cold. It reaches the dark waters of the lake as it spills across. From within the fog she hears loud screams. Susan turns to run and yells, ***"No, No!"*** While running to find the garden, she looks for a way out! She realizes she is lost. She stops running. Frantically overwhelmed with fear everything around her begins to spin. Her eyes fall upon three women sitting on the ground in front of some trees a couple of feet away from her, one to her right, one to her left and another in the front. They sit with their legs crossed with their heads bowed down. Susan quickly jolts to run around them.

Suddenly, they all lift their heads all at once. Susan stops. Their faces are pale white. Their eyes are closed shut. The head and arms on the woman to her right begins to rattle violently as she cries out in pain. The one in front begins to pound the back of her head against a tree. Slowly rising out of the ground Susan's eyes open wide in terror as she, witnesses two rattling heads come out of the earth wailing at the woman.

"Susan!" Susan hears a voice calling out to her. She slowly turns to her left staring with her lifeless blind stare, motionless. The woman sitting to her left has her head slanted to her right, breathing heavily as she smiles wickedly.

Suddenly, Susan feels someone standing behind her. Frightened of whom or what it might be, she slowly turns ready to deal with the impact. Standing behind her, is Peter. His face is tired and beaten. Michael steps from behind a nearby tree.

Susan scared asks him with a shaken voice, ***"Who are you, where am I?"*** Michael steps towards her, Susan steps back. Peter answers her question, ***"My name is Peter, you ask where are you?"*** Peter looks up to the sky that slowly transforms into night. He looks back at Susan saying, ***"Believe it or not, this is the place that God has cast off from his sight. This place is for those who have died along with those who have tormented lives. These are the people that were not saved from their oppressors."*** Susan confused answers disturbingly, ***"What are you talking about?"*** Michael shaking says, ***"Maybe you passed on and you did not know you died. With your demons, this is one of the places that Hell has for those who died with their demons."*** Michael begins to tremble violently, ***"It will all soon begin."***

Susan's eyes swell with tears, ***"What?"*** She asks desperately. The fog creeps around them. Everything turns dark. Chains shoot out of the ground wrapping around Peter and Michael's bodies. They begin to sink into the earth screaming and crying. Chains on the necks of the three women lift them. They pull them up into the trees. The chains swing around the branches as their bodies hang swinging side to side, they shake violently screaming in pain and crying out to God. Susan terrified turns around not knowing where to run. The peaceful garden transforms into a nightmare. The lake changes into a bed of fire. Rising out of the ground are souls wrapped in bloody chains screaming and crying. Demons rise out of the ground reaching for them pulling them back into the earth. Others are feasted on. Susan's eyes are blinded by the horror. Everything begins to spin, feeling dizzy and disoriented. Suddenly, a chain wraps around her body spinning her around. Standing before her is a demon looking at her. Susan cries as the chains pull her down to the ground. Her body hits the earth hard as the demon begins to drag her into the flames. The air grows with torturing screams of burning souls lamenting within the fire. Susan cries, screaming and struggling to set herself free as she fades away slowly into the flames.

Hell is an environment that is real. It is real for some. Hell is pure pain. It can exist in the mind of those who became slaves of evil. It is beyond the understanding of the human mind. There is no glory, just suffering. A sad end to many. All around are suffering bodies tormented by their tortures. Similar to savage animals ripping and tearing flesh while fighting over human remains. Many will beg for death, but there is no death in Hell, just pain for all eternity. This is a demon's feeding ground. There are mutilated bodies everywhere. Many cry because of the horror they see. Chanting voices repeat over and over, ***"Sinner! Sinner!"***

A young man in a straight jacket sits in a padded room, rocking himself back and forth while weeping in torment. He looks up and his eyes open wide as he sees what no one else sees. The horror that his mind dwells in. He hears coming out from the burning ground piercing deafening screams. In his cell, a sickening stench of rotting flesh grows. He cries out in anguish, ***"Save me God, save me!"*** In the midst of the horror ghoulish demons stand in front of them looking up to the dark skies above as the fallen one is cast out of grace, burning in this forsaken place.

From inside the house, Susan watches the paramedics placing the stretcher on which her body lies into the ambulance. She sees her parents stepping into the ambulance with her. Father O'Leary with Father James wait to follow the medics. Her mother grief stricken holds Susan's hands. Her Father has his hands on his face sobbing. As medics close the doors, they hear a frightful scream from inside the house. They look at each other and turn quickly to get into the truck. From inside the house, Susan watches as they drive away. Suddenly, the house becomes cold. Behind her, Susan hears gasping sounds and heavy rasping. She closes her eyes. Stepping out from the darkness, her demons approach…

Two days later

In Susan's dorm room, Mrs. Martin and Mr. Martin gather her things. While sealing a box Mrs.

Martin turns to Mr. Martin and says, ***"We should sell the house and start looking for a new place to live after the funeral."*** She notices Mr. Martin holding a book sobbing in the middle of the room by himself as he reads it. She walks towards him, takes the book gently from his hands and closes the book to see what he is reading. On it's cover, it reads, ***My Diary.*** Mr. Martin walks over to what once was Susan's bed and sits looking sadly around the room. On her desk are pictures of Susan and her friends. There were photos of her with her parents last summer. Her mother opens the diary and begins to read what her daughter has left behind. One, two, tear drops fall on the page as she reads. As she reads on, in her mind, she imagines Susan reading with her...

Mom, Dad:

I always wondered what really happened to me when I was younger, that time that the family never talks about. It feels like a part of me is missing, locked in a dark dream. I can't remember what it was. Whatever it was is a question that lingers in my mind. Your sweet lies sheltered me from the dark truth of the thing that I brought forth. I see the reason why you never wanted to tell me. As I write in my dairy, they find pleasure tormenting me. I am frightened. I should never have wished to "find out". My curiosity brought this hell upon me. Everyday, every night is filled with anguish. My life does not belong to me. Pray for me Mother, pray that God may find mercy and save me from this that taunts me. "They are back, and this time your prayers cannot save me." I fear for my life. Just in case I never get the chance to come home, at least you know what happened.

It was a rainy dark day late in the afternoon at the corner of Broad and King Streets, in the city of Elizabeth. There stands a cathedral called St. Catherines. People step off a bus at a nearby bus stop across the street from the cathedral. They cross the street and the bus drives away. Standing and looking at the cathedral is a young man that looks up with swollen eyes. The rain falls against his face and his long brown wet hair falls onto his face. As he crosses the street he walks up to the doors of the church and looks behind him before opening the church doors. There is no one around. Yet, he hears whispering voices and his eyes swell with tears. He opens the doors and enters. The doors close slowly behind him. The church is dark, lit only by a few candles. He looks around and begins to walk slowly down the center aisle towards the altar.

He reaches the altar and lifts his eyes to the crucifix hanging in front of him. He kneels and begins to weep. His cries echo throughout the dark church. The young man hears a strange gasping sound behind him, from the dark corners of the church. He hears more sounds of laughter and whispers. He turns to see what it is but there is nothing there. He looks around, turns and begins to pray. Once again he hears the whispers and voices calling out his name, ***"Glenn."*** He turns and notices down the dark aisle several human form demonic creatures kneeling and whispering. Glenn looks down at his right arm. It begins to shake violently out of control. He panics from the pain. The church is filled with a foul stench. The beasts heads began to jolt violently, one of them stands up and with a sudden halt its head stops rattling. A rasping voice spoke out and says, ***"You will not find sanctuary here."*** They all stand up around the church and it fills with laughter. Slowly, it turns into tormenting screams. Glenn cries out, ***"Please leave me alone I can't take it anymore."*** No answer came from them. Glenn falls to his knees. He began to feel sick. He hears a cracking sound. He looks up to the statues of the saints and their heads turn to him staring.

Suddenly, screams came out from them. Glenn goes to cover his ears and suddenly a chain wraps around his neck! Unaware, Glenn realizes he is now in his own bed back in his room with his eyes open. While he was dreaming he was soaked from his own sweat and he started breathing heavily. He wakes from his nightmare, out of breath. He tries to call out to his wife Karen who is in the kitchen downstairs. Glenn, frightened and frozen, is in shock by the dark shadowy figures that he sees standing before him. They are now in his bedroom! Across from him one of them rise from the rocking chair and walks slowly towards him. Glenn screams. Karen hears his screams from downstairs. She quickly runs upstairs and rushes into the bedroom to see Glenn with his hands covering his eyes. Karen quickly walks up to him and says, ***"I'm here Glenn!"*** She sits by him and gently puts her arms around him. He cries like a frightened child. He hugs his wife weeping and says, ***"I'm so tired of these God forsaken dreams!"*** She comforts him by caressing his hands and face with her hands. Glenn hears a voice, ***"It's just getting started."*** Glenn's eyes fill with tears.

The following day

Glenn stops by Dr. Bell's office for a psychiatric evaluation. Glenn walks into the office. Sitting behind the desk is Dr. Bell who says, ***"Good morning Glenn."*** Glenn closes the door behind him and says, ***"How are you doing Dr. Bell?"*** He sits down. Dr. Bell says, ***"Karen spoke to me before you came in and told me you had another one of your episodes. Still seeing images?"*** Glenn replies, ***"Yes."*** He sits with his hands covering his face. He then slowly lifts up his head and looks at Dr. Bell saying, ***"I want you to understand something Dr.*** (He pauses) ***okay? The images that I see are not only in my dreams, not only when I am asleep, but also when I am awake. I see these frightening images, they scare me, okay? Sometimes I***

feel and hear them around me but I don't always see them. It is hard to explain my situation. They taunt me. When I am alone at home. When I am at work I sense an unpleasant presence over me. Like a cold chill. I have no words to describe what is happening to me. I am terrified! They hurt me. The things that you see upon my body are impossible for me to inflict on myself. These scratches, bruises and bite marks.." Glenn shows Dr. Bell by lifting up his sweater. Dr. Bell leans forward, takes off his glasses slowly and stands walking towards Glenn. He examines the marks on Glenn's battered body. He also notices hand impressions in his neck. Dr. Bell with a puzzled expression walks back to his desk and sits down.

"In the beginning it was insomnia, like I could not sleep. I felt uncomfortable constantly and restless. Before all this got out of control, I felt a constant

presence. That's the only way I can explain it. That made me feel consistently fearful even when I would go to sleep at night. I felt this unimaginable fear in the depths of my soul. I felt it on my skin. It would make me feel sick to the point that I would throw up. Doctor did you ever feel so afraid that the hairs on the back of your neck would stand up? It was as if someone poured cold water down your neck. I would feel something behind me, staring right at me, and when I would turn around to see what it was, there would be nothing there! It was around this time when I would hear giggles, voices taunting me endlessly. Dr. I need you! Please try to help me. If you only knew what I am going through! I come to you because you study the mind and how it works. Help me to understand why these things are happening. How much longer do I have to wait for

answers, before I am continuously examined and probed? You and Dr. Iglesias keep going back and forth to each other and still have no answers. It seems to me that you guys are going through a never-ending maze and it shows on your faces that you are doubtful! Do you feel like you have no clues how to diagnose me? Is it schizophrenia or an unexplainable disorder?"

Tears fall from his eyes as he repeats, ***"I see terrifying things, it's not only the dreams."***

Dr. Bell watches how Glenn expresses himself, how frustrated and desperate he is. Dr. Bell listens to all that Glenn says to him and he remembers his past sessions. He is not sure what to make out of all of this, if indeed it's a mental illness. Then, what would explain the marks on Glenn's body? Dr. Bell sometimes doubts that what Glenn is suffering from is an illness or whether he could be inflicting these wounds on himself.

Glenn continues on to say, ***"Dr. Bell, I'm paying you to hear me out, I don't want you to think I am some kind of nut. I lost my job at the plant, God I don't know how much more of this I can take. I have no idea when this sourness began. I never had problems like this before, not even breakdowns or ever taken medications for anything. This is the first time in my life I am being evaluated by psychiatrists like yourself! You have no idea what it's like living in this nightmare. When your eyes are open you are wide-awake but it seems like your still dreaming. I can't differentiate between being asleep and being awake anymore."***

Dr. Bell sits up in front of him on his desk and looks through Glenn's medical file. He says to

Glenn, ***"When you first came to us you explained to Dr. Iglesias about a sleeping disorder you had been experiencing."*** He pauses as he searches through his notes and flips to the next page of his file. Glenn continues to say, ***"Dr. I don't believe in the Devil or in God but to my understanding what I see calling out to me are demons. My nights are filled with tormenting screams. These things find so much pleasure in watching me suffer! You know what Dr.? I am not sure but I think there are others like myself! I see them. The pain they endure! I see myself standing in a peaceful place, like a garden hidden by thick fog. This garden is not a place of peace. It seems that way at first when you enter it. But it is really a place of pain and torment, it deceives you!"***

"Who are these others? Are the people?" Asks Dr. Bell.

Glenn replies, ***"I don't know them and I don't understand why they are in my dreams. Some of them were alive, now they are in this dark and torturous place. For example, there is a young man locked away somewhere but I don't know where! What I do know is that he is suffering! Demons feast on his tormented mind."***

Dr. Bell asks Glenn, ***"Have you any idea who these people are?"***

Glenn nods no. Dr. Bell asks Glenn, ***"Is there anything else you want to tell me?"***

Glenn replies, ***"No Dr."***

"Are you sure? Glenn, here is what we are going to do. We are going to run some tests, an MRI and a CAT scan to rule out any malignant tumors. Studies and research prove that individuals with growing tumors

have or experience constant or occasional dilusional episodes. I am going to talk this through with Dr. Mark. He is a doctor at St. James Hospital in Newark. After the evaluation exam with Dr. Mark we will take it from there. I am setting up the appointments for the tenth. What's good for you? The morning or the afternoon?"

Glenn nods yes to the morning as being better for him.

Dr. Bell hands Glenn the appointment card saying, ***"Here you go, the appointment is for 11AM. Here is my cell phone number, if you need me call me!***

Glenn says, ***"Thank you Dr."*** He stands up and so does Dr. Bell. They shake hands. Glenn turns and walks across the room out the office.

Later that night

Glenn is at home by himself. He is up in his study writing on his computer. Glenn hears something downstairs. Someone is knocking on the front door. The knocks become loud bangs! Glenn gets up from his chair. He walks out into the hall and down the stairs. As he walks down the stairs, the bangs become louder, faster and out of control. Glenn quickly reaches for the doorknob and the banging suddenly stops. He pauses, puzzled he opens the door and there is no one there. He feels uncomfortable and senses an unpleasant presence overcoming him! He closes the door. Slowly he walks towards the stairs. He feels a chill. He stops, looks back and notices shadows moving beneath the door. He also hears screeching noises against the door. He slowly walks over to it but notices from out the window at the front of the house that there is someone at the door. There is a knock and another knock, finally Glenn turns and looks at the door angrily. He walks to it and swings it wide open yelling, ***"What the fu…Karen?"***

Startled, Karen says frightened, ***"God Glenn! You almost gave me a heart attack!"***

Glenn looks outside and steps back into the house closing the door behind them. He walks into the living room.

"What was all that about?"

"I was upstairs working and I heard a constant banging on the door!" It was out of control, and loud. That's when I rushed down here and opened the door, I'm sorry if I scared you!

Karen walks over to him and puts her arms around him. She kisses him and he smiles. Karen looks into his eyes seductively and says to him, ***"I'm going upstairs to take a nice hot bath! After the bath I will give you a stress reliever like you have never had!"***

Glenn kisses her gently. Karen walks up the stairs slowly taking off her blouse and dropping it on the stairs. As she does this Glenn watches her. She reaches the top of the steps and walks down the hall into the bathroom. Glenn turns off the light and walks upstairs. He walks into his study. Karen is in the bathroom filling up the bathtub with water. Glenn shuts off his computer and turns off the lights. Outside Glenn can hear the wind howling. Glenn walks out and looks down the hall, he does not feel right. He walks across the hall into the bedroom. He walks over to the bed and sits on it taking off his clothes. After he gets ready for bed he stands, pulls the covers back and lays on the bed with his eyes closed.

Minutes later, Karen walks into the bedroom and sees Glenn sleeping peacefully. She walks over to turn off the lights and slips into bed gently, without disturbing him. Karen lays her head upon his chest and closes her eyes.

Late into the night as they slept

Glenn is awakened by a loud piercing scream. Startled by the scream he lifts up his head and turns to Karen. She is sound asleep! He turns his head towards the door. Slowly it opens and he feels a cold draft coming from it. He hears whispering voices saying softly over and over again, ***"Satanas".***

Glenn slowly steps out of bed and walks towards the door. Behind him, he hears a heavy gasping sound. He turns his eyes open wide with fear as he sees Karen sitting on the edge of the bed with her legs crossed. Her long blond hair covers her face and wicked smirk.

"Karen?" Glenn whispers out to her. Karen's eyes roll white!

Suddenly, Glenn wakes up breathing heavily. He turns to Karen. She's looking at him. She sits up and says ***"Babe? Are you okay?"*** She puts her hand on him and leans over to comfort him. Glenn sobs and says, ***"Oh God."*** He rolls over on his side with his back facing Karen. She sits up watching him cry. Her eyes fill with tears as she moves closer to him.

Days pass by

Glenn goes to check up on his results. He is sitting in Dr. Bell's office discussing them.

Dr. Bell says, ***"Well Glenn the test results came in and the cat-scan shows that your brain waves are as normal as any other person. The images of your brain X-ray show no growing tumors. Your blood work and MRI results also came back normal. All your psychiatric evaluations are somewhat, not completely normal! There is one thing. You do suffer from high levels of stress and depression! This alone increases the chances of you experiencing these delusions. Stress alone Glenn is the result of other pressures that have been shown to significantly alter, deform and distort one's psychological health. These delusions brought on by stress and lead to constant depression which are***

persistent. This would explain how they show up anywhere, at home, work, on the street, asleep or awake. Now, the dreams, that is one thing we have to talk about. Have you been taking the medication?" Understand Glenn that without the medication the delusions can take over your life! You have to follow the tx or the delusions become part of reality for you!

Glenn restless turns to Dr. Bell not making any sense says to him, ***"Your pills are not helping! When I do take them they make me sick and I feel dumb and slow! And I don't think they help the delusions go away. It's not me and my life is falling apart!***

Dr. Bell watches Glenn's unsettled reaction, expressing himself with anger as he says to him, ***"I'm telling you I can't live like this anymore!"***

He has dark purple bruises, scratches and bite marks all over. They seem to have gotten worse. Glenn peels off the bandages covering the bite marks on his back. Dr. Bell stands up from his chair and looks at them. Glenn pulls down his sweater and sits. Dr. Bell walks back to his chair shocked. Glenn goes on to say to him, ***"What explanation does modern medicine have for these marks on my body? It is impossible for me to have inflicted them on myself! Dr. forgive me for what I'm about to say but I don't think that you can help me. This has nothing to do with you. I've been through three weeks of test and a computer that reads nothing! Everything that you say I have the stress the depression, I know! I'm paying you to find the answers to what is happening to me. In reality you don't have those answers, do you?"*** Glenn sadly stands from his chair shaking nervously.

Dr. Bell stands from his chair and says, ***"So you're just going to give up? Not give us a chance? At least we should find the answers for what's happening to you together! I want to find out more about what's making this happen to you! Please, I want to help you! There has to be a way to help you!***

Glenn walks to the door with tears in his eyes. Hearing voices he turns to Dr. Bell and sees Dr. Bell's eyes roll white! He speaks out to him in multiple voices, ***"Weep for us Glenn!"***

Glenn closes his eyes scared and slowly opens them again, he sees Dr. Bell standing as himself and Glenn says to the Dr., ***"It's a bad dream you can't wake me up from!"*** Glenn opens the door and walks out. Dr. Bell stands watching as the office door slowly closes. Glenn walks out of the building and over to the parking deck. He begins to walk up the parking deck stairs to the 3rd level. He hears voices calling out from behind him. He stops and turns and sees nothing! He continues to walk up another level.

Glenn hears his name called out again, ***"Glenn!"*** He turns around once again and sees nothing! But again he hears his name called out, ***"Glenn, Glenn, Glenn!"*** Glenn covers his ears. Running he yells out, ***"Stop!"***

Silence surrounds Glenn and he uncovers his ears. He quickly walks towards his car to get in when suddenly behind him something approaches him rapidly! A great force pushes him down to the ground and quickly drags him towards his car. Before reaching it an unseen force lifts him up off the ground and slams him against the hood of his car! Glenn hurt and disoriented drops to the ground.

From a distance he hears sounds of shattered glass approaching him! He looks up and sees that all the cars' windows are being smashed! Leading towards him! Glenn quickly gets up from the floor limping. He opens his car door and quickly gets in turning the ignition on. He manages to drive away going down level after level. The cars' windows shatter all around him! Glenn drives faster towards the exit. He slows down noticing behind him nothing happening! He approaches the deck attendant and Glenn rolls down his window to hand him his ticket. As he gives it to the attendant the man asks him, ***"Sir, are you ok."***

Glenn pale and sweating looks up to the attendant who looks like a kind, old man. He says out of breath, ***"Yes, I'm okay!"***

"Four dollars please." Glenn pays the old man who then says, ***"Thank you, Glenn."***

Glenn turns to the old man stunned that he knew his name. He then drives away slowly getting a glimpse of the old man through his rear view mirror, he sees the old man sticking out his tongue demonically at him!

That night

It is cold and the rain is tapping on the window glass. Glenn is sitting with Karen in the living room in front of the fire. As they are warming themselves up Glenn turns to Karen and says, ***"Karen, don't ever leave me!"*** Karen looks at him as he tells her this. He continues, ***"I'm sorry for all this!"***

She leans towards him and says, ***"I will always be by your side until the end! You have me and never think that I'm going to leave you! Together we will make it through this. Never think that again. Okay?"*** She hugs him. As she comforts him she tells him, ***"Glenn Dr. Bell called, you should go back to him, you never know."***

Glenn nodding no says, ***"You don't get it! The more they run tests, the more they are going to think that it is me! These doctors will lock you up in a padded room and throw away the key if they can't find the answers they want! I know I have to find an answer. On the way home today I passed by St.Catherines Church. I went to go see Father Thomas. I stopped in and he was surprised to see me. He has known me since I was a kid. I told him that I had to talk to him, that I was very***

troubled. I asked him when would be a good time to speak to him to let him know what was going on with me. He said that when I had a chance to come in, the doors would always be open!

If I can't find what I'm looking for with Father Thomas, I don't know what I'm going to do. I hope he can help me find peace!"

Glenn stands up from his chair and slowly walks over to the fireplace. There he squats down looking deep into the flames. Within the flames, he hears softly torturous screams. Karen watches him speechless and feels helpless because she can't do anything to help her husband. She walks towards him and sits beside him.

As the days passed

Glenn's condition got worse and Karen felt even more useless! Karen continued watching Glenn being tormented and all she could do was to try to comfort him and be understanding. Day by day, night by night the things that were happening to Glenn didn't just get worse, they got violent!

Late into the night as they slept, Karen began to dream that she herself was running away from someone who was trying to kill her. Suddenly, she saw herself struggling, fighting for her life on the floor, as the killer was on top of her holding her down with great force. She feels herself being stabbed repeatedly. The man's head in her dream was jarring violently. Deep within this nightmare she tried to scream, ***"Glenn!"*** She couldn't hear herself scream! Suddenly, she wakes up breathing heavily and frightened by what she was dreaming.

She turns to Glenn. He is on the floor in a dark corner, weeping. He calls out her name softly, ***"Karen?"*** His head is leaned over between his legs, he calls out to her again.

Karen replies, ***"What wrong?"***

Glenn slowly looks up, his eyes are closed, and he trembles saying, ***"help me Karen!"***

He opens his eyes as he screams! Tears fall from his eyes, he sobs saying, ***"there are so many of them!"*** His eyes roll white! Karen begins to cry, terrified she starts calling out, ***"Glenn!"*** He stands and says, ***"Why is this happening to me?"*** From his mouth a gasping voice speaks out, ***"salvation will not save him!"*** Glenn passes out on the floor. Karen jumps out of bed and runs over to him. She holds him calling out his name, ***"Glenn, Glenn baby!"*** His eyes open disoriented. He begins to weep, holding onto Karen. The room darkens with Glenn's cries.

Morning Came

Glenn walks out of his house. It is a cold and gray day. He looks up before walking down the steps. It is also breezy. He lifts up the collar of his coat and walks down the front steps. He walks a few blocks to catch the bus at the corner stop.

Karen is at Dr. Bell's office talking about Glenn and what happened last night! She tries to make Dr. Bell understand that Glenn is not sick. She lets him know that her husband is being tormented by something that has nothing to do with mental illness or self inflicted torture. She deeply believes that it has to do with something evil! She pauses and thinks for a moment and then says, ***"I might sound silly or off the wall but I have been going to bookstores looking for books to help me learn about Glenn's problem. I'm so desperate because I want to help him! He has been going to doctors like yourself for quite some time now ever since these nightmares began and there has been no improvement or cure for what he is suffering from. Dr. his condition is getting worse! That is why I wonder if it could be something else? Here are the books that perhaps have some clues to help solve what Glenn is going through."*** She reaches for her bag and pulls out three books. One of them is religious. She hands them to Dr. Bell. As he reaches for them she lays them on his desk. One of the books is titled, "**Know the Enemy**". He looks up to her and says, ***"Mrs. Harris you know that these books are misleading. There are no such things as demons. I***

completely understand how you feel and the position you are in to try and help Glenn. But you have to give us (the doctors) a chance to help Glenn ourselves! His case is one that is very complicated and does require a lot of time and effort. I don't disagree that it could perhaps be something like you have just explained to me but we should rule out all other possibilities! We need to let medicine help figure out what is happening to Glenn!

Karen says to him, ***"But Dr., I'm telling you it's more than that, you haven't seen the things that I have witness happen to him, terrifying things. It's as if he is possessed!***

Meanwhile

Glenn crosses the street and walks over to the bus stop. While he is waiting there, he sees a man. He walks over to the man and asks him, ***"Excuse me Sir did the 10 o'clock bus pass yet?"*** The man turns towards Glenn, looks at him, smiles and walks away! Glenn watches the rude man walk away. Glenn looks behind him at the road and sees cars pass by. He turns and notices that the man has vanished! Glenn holds his head, takes a deep breath and begins to walk up the street towards Dr. Bell's office.

Dr. Bell highly recommends that Glenn come back to seek help. He lets Karen know by saying, ***"Mrs. Harris I don't want to scare you but you should know by the way Glenn reacted in my office the other day that,*** (Pausing, he continues to say) ***In many cases people who have this type of illness can come to a***

point where they see themselves trapped! They can hurt themselves or their loved ones. I would like to talk to him before he gets to that point. I also want to help him."

Glenn walks down the street looking down as people pass him by. As he looks up he stares at them. Their faces have smirks on them. Their eyes are rolled back white. Some of their heads are shaking. Glenn closes his eyes and then opens them. He then notices people just passing him by normal looking. He runs up to a bus stop. As a bus pulls around the corner, it stops. Glenn reaches the line then waits to get on. Glenn wipes his saddened eyes and steps into the bus. He walks down the aisle and sits by a window. He feels something approaching him from behind, he turns and notices a couple of high school kids sitting in the back of the bus talking with one another. Glenn turns back facing the front of the bus and closes his eyes. The bus driver speaks out through the intercom saying, ***"Next stop St. George Avenue."*** Glenn sees Echo Park getting closer. He presses the stop request buzzer and walks towards the front of the bus. As the bus slowly stopped, Glenn steps out of the bus and walks across the street from the park. The bus drives off. He walks across the street through the gates of the park. Glenn remembers how as a child he played with his mother. He reaches the parks lake. A foggy mist floats slowly over it. He walks to a bench that faces the lake. He sits his exhausted body down. His hair rests over his face. It reflects the sadness growing in him. He opens his eyes. Drained out of hope, he relaxes gazing upon the lake watching the foggy mist slowly creeping toward him. The cold winds of winter blow. Glenn snuggles into his coat. His head leans to one side, he watches the lake. Its cold dark waters are still, serene and lifeless. Glenn's eyes swell with tears, as his mouth grows moist. He watches the fog drawing closer. Tears fall from his eyes. Within the fog, something moves slowly. Glenn focuses. He can see them walking towards him. They are walking over the water within the fog. As it draws near they get closer, demonic human form ghouls dressed in black robes. A cold breeze blows the fog over them slowly as they disappear within the lake. Chilling screams echo and fade with laughter into the mist.

Later that afternoon Glenn stops by Dr. Bell's office unexpectedly. Dr. Bell's secretary is surprised to see Glenn walking in through the doors and says, ***"Mr. Harris, good afternoon."*** Glenn replies, ***"Hello***

Jane, is Dr. Bell in? I would like to see him if possible, please." Jane stands and asks Glenn to wait one moment. She goes down the hall to knock on Dr. Bell's door. Glenn stands in the middle of the waiting room watching Jane walk into the office. Glenn begins to hear the tormenting laughter in his mind.

Glenn closes his eyes as Dr. Bell walks out of his office to greet him and says, ***"Glenn."*** As Dr. Bell calls out to him, Glenn opens his eyes and smiles. He walks up to Dr. Bell. Dr. Bell notices the exhausted saddened appearance Glenn has as he passes him by. Glenn walks into the office. He closes the door behind him. Glenn walks over and sits on a chair in front of Dr. Bell's desk.

Dr. Bell says, ***"You know that I spoke to your wife and.."*** Glenn interrupts saying, ***"Dr. I came here***

knowing that you had spoken to my wife, I appreciate your concern. I am here to apologize. I need your help, because I can't continue on like this."

Dr. Bell walks towards his desk listening to what Glenn is saying to him, ***"In the first place you do not need to apologize to me, I understand. Yes, you're not giving me a chance to explain. You are leaving me with my words in my mouth. I never give up anything without trying my best. I do want to help you understand completely that whatever is tormenting you is driving you insane. Nevertheless, I need to work with you to find out if it is an illness or if it is something that is oppressing you. I, as a doctor have to go by logic and research. I believe what you are going through and I want you to know I have concluded that yes, you are suffering from paranoia schizophrenia"*** (Glenn nods no, not wanting to accept what Dr. Bell is saying.) Dr. Bell looks up and sees the discontent in Glenn's face and says, ***"Glenn this does not mean the end, we finally found what we've been searching for. Now we know what we're dealing with and together we can find a way out of this dark tunnel."*** Glenn's ears fill with laughter and mockery. Glenn replies, ***"You think you know what your dealing with but you have no clue what's been happening in my life!*** Glenn stands up. Dr. Bell looks at him wondering where he is going. Glenn walks out saying, ***"This is useless!"***

Glenn is in his living room

He is staring at the flames burning the wood in the fireplace. Karen is in the kitchen cooking. Glenn closes his exhausted eyes. He falls asleep. He begins to dream. He sees himself sitting in the living room with Karen by his side sharing happy joyous moments together with friends and loved ones. They are laughing and talking. Glenn turns and looks to Karen. She is not there. He turns towards his friends and sees everyone standing looking down where Glenn and Karen were. He couldn't understand what was going on so he stood up and walked slowly over to where everyone was. Glenn looks at their faces. They were horrified! They just stood there looking down. Glenn walks between them to see what they were looking at. What he sees blinds him with fear. Shocked, he suddenly sees his friend's heads rattling violently! Glenn drops to his knees. Before him, lying on the floor badly beaten was Karen who lay lifeless on the floor. The clothes on her body were bloody and ripped off. Her eyes were open. She suddenly turned her head towards him with tears rolling down her beaten face.

Glenn is awakened by a frightening scream. He leans over out of breath soaked in sweat. He weeps, rubbing his eyes. He says to himself, "I want this to end. I want my life back, just my life back!" In front of him, a chair moves towards him and stops. He feels something walking behind him. He turns and sees nothing. He feels it next to him. He turns to his right, and then to his left, he still sees nothing. The living room becomes cold. He feels the presence of something sitting in front of him.

Glenn quickly stands up and kicks the chair over. Karen hears a loud thump from the kitchen. Glenn screams. She runs out of the kitchen. Glenn yells out, ***"What the fu..do you want with me? What? Kill me already! Come on what are you waiting for!***

Suddenly, the telephone beside him drops to the floor. The telephone cord is yanked from the socket and begins to whip Glenn! It whips him with great force. Glenn falls to his knees and Karen screams out to Glenn as she sees something unseen whipping him. She attempts to help him. Then suddenly she is thrown against the wall. She falls to the floor. Glenn begs as he is beaten, kicked and whipped. Karen sees something that grabs his shirt. It picks him up and punches him in his face. It drops him. Glenn's head hits the floor. The beatings stop! The room fills up with a foul stench. Within the room they hear fading tortured screams. Glenn slowly uncovers his head. His eyes look around. Karen goes and crawls towards him. He is lifted up in the air and thrown against the wall! His body falls on a corner table dropping the lamp to the ground.

The lights go out. Karen quickly crawls to Glenn holding him in her arms. Images of human form shadows begin to appear in the dark entrance of the living room.

"Let me see tears", says a voice from the shadowy figures. Glenn yells out in agony, ***"What have I done to deserve this!"*** The shadows step forward turning into images of demons. These human form demons reply, ***"Watching you weep pleasures us. Nothing can stop this. Hell waits for you. This is just the beginning of the oppression. You say you are a slave. That you feel the chains that bind you."*** The room fills with screams as other demonic figures step out of the dark corners. Glenn begins to tremble. Stuttering, Glenn calls out, ***"Ka, Ka, Karen."*** Karen is paralyzed with fear. Glenn turns around. His eyes roll white and he stands. The living room grows cold. A mist comes out of his mouth. Glenn screams out her name, ***"Karen!"*** She looks up at him. Her eyes open with terror. Glenn's head begins to rattle viciously. He begins to speak in strange tongues. Glenn yells out, ***"Run, save yourself Karen, go!"*** Glenn screams out in pain as his body is lifted up in the air. Karen drags herself to the front door crying. She is in shock. Karen makes an effort to stand up and run out the front door. It slams shut behind her with a scream. She runs down the street. She stops and notices that she has the car keys in her pocket. She turns and runs back, as she reaches the house, there is silence within it. She cries out, not wanting to leave Glenn behind. She rushes to the car and drives off. Inside the house Glenn stands before demons. Their lifeless white eyes stare at him with a hollow coldness.

Suddenly, Glenn hears loud deafening screams. Glenn covers his ears. Everything around him begins to spin. Glenn shuts his eyes. All of a sudden there is silence. He opens them and realizes he is not home! He sees himself standing before tall dark gates. Behind him, the sunlight slowly dies and darkness falls upon the mountains. The wounded skies reflect signs of no hope. Despair and fear begin to grow within him. Slowly fog begins to flow around him. Glenn starts to feel uncomfortable as if someone is watching him from behind. He can't tell what lies behind the gates. The fog is too thick. He hears voices whispering from behind them. Glenn takes a step forward and sees nothing. However, he does feel the presence of something unpleasant. Deep inside Glenn knows that they are there waiting, lurking in the midst of the fog. Glenn turns back, behind him is an empty blackness. Suddenly, the gates open with piercing cries. Glenn turns and drops to the ground on his knees, covering his ears. Just like that, there is silence once again. Glenn opens his eyes, slowly lifts up his head, and sees the gates opening. Glenn stands up and approaches them stopping at the entrance. He hears voices calling out his name, ***"Glenn."*** He turns because he feels something creeping behind him. He sees that there is nothing, only the empty darkness. He turns to the gates. He closes his eyes, lifts up his leg, takes a deep breath, and steps beyond the gates. As his foot hits the moist ground, he opens his eyes. The fog suddenly begins to drift back into the wet earth with the anguished cries fading into the mist.

Meanwhile, Karen stops at a diner in a nearby town, La Copa. She parks her car in the diner's parking lot. Before stepping out of the car, she wipes the tears from her face. She takes a deep breath and breaks down crying, ***"Oh God, Glenn!"*** She sobs and steps out of the car. As Karen walks up the steps she hears a gasping sound. She turns, there is nothing. She looks around, wipes a tear from her right eye and turns to the door to enter. She reaches into her pocket and pulls out change for the pay phone. She puts the money in and dials the number. On the other end a woman's voice answers and says, ***"Hello?"***

"Mom, it's me, Karen. Listen I'm coming over!"

Her mother on the other end says, ***"What's wrong dear?"***

"I'll explain later, okay? She hangs up. Karen pauses for a moment trying to remember Dr. Bell's number. She puts money in and dials. On the other end the phone rings and rings. Just before she hangs up she hears, ***"Hello?"***

Karen retracts the phone back to her ear and says, ***"Dr. Bell, it's me Karen."***

"Oh hi."

"Dr. Bell it's Glenn, oh God he.."

Glenn slowly begins to see a garden filled with burning candles as the fog clears. Within the garden are beautiful detailed statues of angels crying and one of a young maiden in distress. There is one that seems to be a man on his knees covering his face with his hands. Time has hidden some of these statues beauty. Glenn walks toward the statues to take a better look. He walks under a tree filled with a flock of ravens that are staring at him. Glenn pays no attention to them. He approaches the statue of the young maiden. As he stands in front of the statue, Glenn feels that it is looking down at him. He gazes into its sad eyes. In his mind, he began to see images of this young woman in a dark eerie place. He can feel her fear, her tormented cries echoing throughout his head. Her face is beaten. Her tired eyes are filled with feelings of despair. Glenn snaps out of this by a sudden deafening scream. He turns as it echoes through the garden. Feeling dizzy he closes and opens his eyes. He walks away from the statue hearing faded screams coming from within it. Behind Glenn, he hears whispering voices. He turns to see bodies all around him hanging from trees by their necks! Their hands and legs bled from the barbwires that were tied around them. Coming out of the ground are bodies wailing as they sink back into the ground, tied against wooden poles with barbwires wrapped around them as well. They rise out again. They begin to shake and tremble as they sink and rise out of the ground. With them rise the demonic lifeless ghouls that begin to torture these poor souls in ways that could make anyone sick. They open their eyes staring at him. Glenn stands terrified by what he is seeing. Their eyes turn white. Glenn, cries out! He hears himself scream but there is no sound coming out of his mouth. When they sink back into the ground Glenn looks around for a way to run. When they rise out again one of the poor souls being tortured speaks out in many voices. It says to Glenn, ***"Witness this place in which you stand it is filled with pain. This is Hell. Welcome to it."*** Glenn looks around. It looks like Hell as demons rise out of the earth to torment the poor souls. There are victims burning while crying in anguish. Glenn questions himself in grief, ***"Can this place be real? Am I living this?"*** There is laughter mixed with screams wherever Glenn sets his eyes upon, he faces the horror of suffering. There are impaled bodies still alive. They scream and cry in pain.

Above them is a tornado of souls swirling, releasing the sounds of millions of cries as something unseen was beating their bodies, causing slash marks and tears. Their bodies are beaten by something else unseen. Demons jumped up from the ground into the air grabbing them and ripping them apart. Some were thrown against the ground and attacked viciously. Standing next to Glenn was an angel, it turned to him and said, ***"Come, quickly follow me."*** Glenn turns to those being feasted upon. Tortured rotten corpses rose from the ground. Their heads were rattling. Glenn begins to step back away from them as they reach for him. He turns and notices that the angel is not by him anymore. He notices from a short distance away that the angel is standing in front of a cathedral. The cathedral is lit up. The angel walks up the steps and stops by the entrance. He opens the doors. Glenn runs quickly toward the cathedral as he sees the angel entering. He runs across a field of impaled bodies that are crying out to him. Above him is a young woman, she screams out to him, ***"Salvate!"***

Glenn turns and trips falling to the ground. The cathedral's bells begin to ring, giving Glenn a sense of dread, no hope and damnation. Glenn, hurt by the fall, holds his legs. He raises his head and gazes at the field of impaled bodies. The young woman looks at him, her eyes rolled back with a cold white stare. She begins to pull out of her body, the impaled rod. She starts speaking in a strange language. Glenn tries to stand up. He notices the young woman's body drop to the ground. Glenn slowly stands shaking. He quickly turns and tries to run with a twisted ankle. He reaches the cathedral and staggers up the steps. Glenn turns back before reaching the door seeing the young woman repeating over and over, ***"salvate!"*** Her voice grows louder and louder. She begins to walk towards Glenn. Every step she takes she draws closer. Behind her is lifeless rotting corpses quickly approaching! Glenn runs up the last step and reaches for the door. The bells of the cathedral suddenly stop ringing. The young woman stops and stands in front of the cathedral's steps. She turns to look behind her and sees the rotting corpses quickly approach her. She turns to Glenn. They reach out to her and push her to the ground. They begin to beat her. Feasting upon her flesh, they suddenly begin to sink into the ground, dragging her with them. Glenn quickly opens the door and rushes in. The door behind him slowly closes. Glenn is now standing at the entrance of the cathedral. The cathedral is lit with candles all around. He sees shadows that move upon its walls. In front of him is a long dark aisle leading to the altar that was also lit by candles. He walks slowly down the cathedral aisle so silently that he can hear himself breathe. The shadows on the wall are moving along with him. Glenn turns to them hearing them whispering all around him. Glenn hears a voice say, ***"You live in question! Isn't it a devastation not to have the answers?"*** He looks over to where the voice is coming from, a dark corner, Glenn questions the voice, ***"What do you want with***

me?" He waits for a response but there is no answer. His ears fill with silence. Glenn looks at the altar, there are six bodies sitting with their legs crossed. Their hands tied behind their backs with their heads covered with black hoods. The cathedral grows cold. Stepping out of the darkness is human like creatures. From their waist down they have hoof legs like a goat and their eyes are sewn shut! The cathedral brightens with screams and the heads of the bodies at the altar begin to shake and rattle so violently that the hoods slowly come off their heads. Then suddenly, their heads stop jarring and their faces reflect despair. Among the six figures on the altar, some had their ears cut off and some had their eyes and mouths sewn shut. (Speak no evil, hear no evil, and see no evil!) Glenn lifts his head and looks up above him. There were bodies dangling upside down by their legs. They were beaten and bleeding. Among those crying were Peter, Linda and Susan! Glenn looks down at the altar, stepping down from it as he sees a ghoulish demon. It was walking towards him. Glenn couldn't move! He was sick because of the foul stench of rotting flesh. As it came closer to him, Glenn began to feel an unpleasant feeling come over him, as if something stepped into his body! His legs became weak and his body began to shake. He raised his head up, opening his eyes as they rolled back. Tears came down from them. He cries out! All around him, tormenting screams came out from the darkness. Deep in the darkness those who burn, those who suffer, all types of race, color, the wicked, liars, unbelievers and even the demented feast upon them with fury. There are inverted crosses in a row with dozens of people being crucified. They are lifted up to the gloomy murky air. Glenn looks down at the seats of the cathedral. Sitting on their knees are poor souls that had their eyelids sewn shut. They cried in pain, ***"Oh my eyes!"*** Others are sitting with their legs crossed lashing themselves with whips! Their heads rattle and they cry aloud. From the multitude was what seemed to be a man in a straight jacket crawling on his knees coming closer to him as his head rattled. He laments in pain. He approaches Glenn and sits in front of him. He speaks out with a shaken voice repeating, ***"Suffer the children!"*** Glenn gazes across the hellish nightmare that he finds himself in. There are people crawling towards him. Some were foaming from their mouths going through convulsions, others, their heads were rattling and they screamed madly while some were lifted up into the air and their bodies dropped into a pit. In this pit are wild crazed demons that attack them viciously tearing them apart! Here in this place you will not find death just eternal torture of souls.

The young man in the straight jacket says, ***"For those that believe in Heaven or Hell, at the end of time, shall all find out won't they?"***

Glenn now able to walk turns around and begins to scream running towards the doors hearing behind him the screams and cries. Peter drops to the floor. He lifts up his head and looks across through the multitude seeing Glenn run to the doors. A chain wraps around his neck and yanks him onto his back dragging him across the ground into the tormenting grounds as his body blends in with the others. Glenn runs down to the bottom of the steps of the cathedral. The door slowly shuts behind him muffling the screams inside. Glenn stands confused not knowing where to run. He looks up to the gray and gloomy sky above. He looks across the field of impaled bodies that are crying in pain. Beyond the rising of bodies and the rotting corpses being feasted upon are the victims crying in anguish. They try to escape from the torture being inflicted upon them. He begins to hear the sound of beating drums with chants. Glenn tries to see where the noise is coming from. He turns to see where the hung bodies were. The fog slowly begins to spill out of the ground quickly where the statues were. From within the fog as it began to flow down towards him, there were figures dressed in black robes chanting across the field of bodies. Some stopped somewhere halfway into the ground as others are out of the ground, helplessly tied to a pole. They watch in terror as the demons slowly walk away, behind the trees. The fog flows over them as Glenn tries to see into the fog to see what is there, but it is too thick. He can only hear horrible cries. Glenn turns to the impaled bodies trying to push the rods out of their bodies. He watches as some are freed of the rod. They drop to the ground in unspeakable pain. They crawl towards him. Glenn turns to see his dragging body along the ground. One of them is Jacob. He is bleeding from his head. The wound was caused by a gunshot. Glenn feels sick. He is afraid that what is inside of him is taking over his body! He sees the fog draw closer and closer. He looks up again to the sky as it turns black. Jacob sits in front of him staring at Glenn, laughing he says to him, ***"This place is filled with insanity my friend!"***

Glenn's body begins to shake and tremble. He throws his head up and screams. Everything around him continues as a nightmarish hell! Images blind him. Screams come from the ground under the bodies of those screaming in pain. They are in anguish beyond belief and the suffering, which the human mind can not conceive or imagine waits for those who walk in the path of disbelief. The path of the wicked, sinners, blasphemers are those who work against the will and the laws of God, the question in everyone's mind is how do we know whether there is a Heaven or Hell? Open your eyes, look around, the truth is right before you!

In the midst of the darkness of the room

Glenn's face turns pale as death. Dr. Bell drives his car up to Glenn's house and into the driveway. Sitting in his car staring at the house he feels uncomfortable. An awful sense comes over him. He steps out of the car and approaches the front of the house. He puts his right foot on the steps. Dr. Bell feels a cold chill come over him as he walks slowly up step by step to the front door. The door was halfway opened when he hears gasping sounds coming from inside the house. Dr. Bell stands in front of the door. He looks behind him. He calls out Glenn's name. His voice echoes. The front door opens more releasing a gasping whispering voice, ***"Satanas!"***

He says in a low voice, ***"Oh God!"***

The door suddenly slams shut with a deafening scream. Dr. Bell jumps back looking at the house.

He turns slowly, walks down the steps and away towards his car. From within the house Glenn is in the darkness watching Dr. Bell get into his car. Glenn smiles wickedly as Dr. Bell drives out the driveway and away from the house.

Glenn is tormented by hellish screams in his head. Suddenly, the front door opens, Glenn slowly walks towards it and steps to the front porch. He covers his head and walks down the steps of the house into the street.

Back at Karen's mother's house

Karen is with her mother crying in her arms. She is so frightened and exhausted! Her mother trying to calm her down shakes her. She is trying to find out what happened. Karen looks up to her and begins to explain what has been going on with Glenn.

Dr. Bell drives down the dark road. He turns on the reading light inside the car to see the directions that Karen gave him over the phone to get to her mother's house.

Back at Karen's mom's house, her mother is shocked by what Karen is telling her, ***"Why didn't you tell me about this?"***

Karen turns to her and says, ***"Oh mom, how did you expect me to tell you something like this, it's something that.."*** The door bell rings interrupting her. Karen's mother gets up from her seat and walks towards the door. She asks before opening the door, ***"Who is it?"***

"It's Dr. Bell, is Karen there please?"

She opens the door and Dr. Bell walks in.

Meanwhile Glenn walks towards downtown Elizabeth. He crosses the street. There are few people walking across the street from the train station. Glenn walks up to a phone and reaches into his pocket pulling out a hand full of change. His hand shakes. He takes 35 cents, trembling, he puts the money in the phone and slowly dials the number. At the other end of the phone a voice answers, ***"Hello?"***

Glenn answers with a shaky voice, ***"Benny it's me, Glenn. I need to see you!"***

"Glenn where are you? Karen called me hysterically and asked me to go by your house to see how you were. I did and you weren't there! Where are you? Tell me I'll come and pick you up!"

Glenn sobbing says, ***"Benny remember what I told you about what's been happening to me? I really need***

to see you. Okay Glenn, tell me where you are, please! Karen is very upset and worried about you!"

Glenn hearing voices in his head, then laughter turning slowly into screams rests his head against the phone and continues onto say, ***"Benny I'm coming over, help me Benny, please help me!"***

Benny on the other end starts to yell out to Glenn, but suddenly, the phone hangs up on the other end. There were two black teenage boys passing by. They see Glenn leaning on the phone and they walk up to him to see if he is all right. They ask him, ***"Excuse me Sir, are you okay?"***

Glenn lifts his head to them when he does he pushes them away. Glenn is terrified. He sees their eyes roll back white with an evil wicked grin on their faces. They walk up to Glenn and say, ***"What's wrong?"***

Glenn screams pointing at them, ***"You keep the fu..away from me, leave me alone!"***

Glenn runs away screaming. The two boys confused say to one another, ***"What the fu.. is wrong with him?"***

Back at Karen's mother's house, Dr. Bell is on the phone talking with the police reporting Glenn as a missing patient who ran away from his home. As Dr. Bell gives the details, the officer on the other end is taking down the information. The officer asks, ***"So he's a patient of yours? Is he mentally ill? Is he dangerous?"***

"Could be, depends on what state of mind he's in." Says Dr. Bell.

"Dr. Bell we will check up on what you reported and send a police car to the house to check if he has

returned, if we have any information we'll get back to you."

"Thank you officer." Dr. Bell hangs up the phone and turns to Karen who is standing by her mother, ***"What did they say?"*** She asked.

"They said they are going to check up on him!"

Glenn walks up to Benny's door and rings the doorbell. The door opens, Glenn looks up to Benny shivering and says, ***"Benny."***

Glenn walks in. Benny is a long time friend. He is an author of New Age Religion and is a spiritualist. Benny closes the door behind him and says, ***"Glenn come over here sit next to the fireplace, warm up. I'm going to get you some warm blankets. Let me get some clothes for you to change into. Get yourself out of those wet clothes, wait here."***

Benny walks up the stairs as Glenn sits by the fireplace trying to warm himself up. He is looking around the living room as Benny walks down the steps and into the living room handing him a nice warm fleece blanket and dry clothes. Benny says, ***"Hey while you change I'll make some hot chocolate."***

Glenn wraps himself up in the blanket. Benny walks over to the kitchen. Glenn gazes into the flames in the fireplace. He changes taking off his wet clothes.

"Hey Ben, remember what I told you about what's been going on with me?"

"Yeah!"

"Listen you know that I don't believe in any of the things that you believe in, but I really need to find a way to stop these things that have been taunting me."

"What do you mean? You want me to help you in what? Tell me, I will help you in any way I can. Oh, just to let you know I called Karen to let her know that you are okay and that you're with me." Benny walks out of the kitchen holding two mugs with hot chocolate. Glenn turns to him asking, ***"Where is she staying?"***

"She's staying with her mother!"

Glenn turns to the fireplace as it burns the wood within its flames. He says to Benny, ***"I know you're into what you call purification's or whatever you do in your rituals. I want you to liberate me from what's oppressing me and driving me insane. You have told me in the past that you can do this. Right?"***

Benny takes a deep breath and says, ***"Yes."***

Benny is what Latin people call a "Brujero." Benny's mother was into "Santeria" in Cuba. Over the fireplace Glenn looks up and sees an old picture of Benny's mother dressed in white. A white bandana was wrapped around her head. Around her neck was a necklace with different colorful beads, ***"Is that your mother?"***

Glenn asks Benny. Benny looks up saying, ***"Yeah, that's my mother, God rest her soul. She died in Cuba four years ago. I never got to see her. My grandmother told me she passed away. The way she died was strange and frightening.***

Glenn asks, ***"What do you mean frightening?"***

Benny continues, ***"I was here in the states with my father. They separated when I was ten. My dad heard from my grandmother that mom was in the last stages of life. It was bizarre. From one day to the next, she fell***

ill with an unexplainable infection. She had a high fever and was in bad shape. When everybody gathered around her bed, my father, grandmother and few other family members, along with friends, said that she had opened her eyes. At the same time my mother's condition made her too weak to speak or move. So my grandmother said that her eyes began to tear. She opened her mouth as to speak but no sound came out. My grandmother said my mother suddenly turned to her and sobbing faintly said, "Why is there a man standing in front of my bed dressed in black?" No one had any idea of what she was talking about plus they could hardly hear her. They thought she was delirious but my grandmother felt an unpleasant presence. My mother turned and stared straight ahead (the dark figure looking down, its head was covered with a black

hood. It slowly lifted its head). She gasped for air. Her eyes roll back and she died as she released her last breath of life staring straight ahead.

In Benny's mind her image slowly fades. Glenn's eyes fill swollen of tears.

"You see, Glenn, when you told me about your problem it reminded me of people I have helped. People with problems such as unclean spirits. I can help you."

Benny stands up from his chair, ***"Listen it's getting late I told Karen that you're going to stay over. You look exhausted. Come, let me show you to your room. We'll talk more tomorrow."***

Glenn follows him across the living room up the stairs. Benny takes Glenn to the room where he is going to spend the night. Benny turns to Glenn and says, ***"If you need anything call me."*** They both shake hands and Glenn tells Benny, ***"Thank you, I appreciate you letting me stay here for the night!"***

Benny smiles and says, ***"Don't worry about it, we'll talk tomorrow."*** Benny walks out the room slowly closing the door behind him. Glenn walks towards the bed and sits down.

Later that night as the grandfather clock struck 1:00 am. Benny is sleeping in his room, Glenn wakes up frightened by a scream. He sits up in bed as the door to the room opens slowly. Within the darkness of the hall Glenn hears voices whispering. His eyes tear. They fall down his cheeks. Glenn gets out of bed and slowly walks out of the bedroom. Glenn walks down the hall towards Benny's room. As Glenn passes by a large room with its door halfway open, he stops and turns to walk into it. The room was filled with statues. Some were like

African saints. There was also a small altar in the room. On the floor there was a basket filled with fruits, which was lit by candle. Upon the altar was a glass cup filled with water and dipped into it was a crucifix. Glenn walks towards the altar, he notices that there is a picture of him. Holding the picture was a small African relic made out of wood. Glenn looks behind him and notices a dark figure of some sort in a dark corner of the room. Glenn couldn't make out what it was. The candles burning behind him cast a long shadow of him along the wall. He notices it's a statue as he slowly approaches it. Then he clearly sees that it is a man-size statue of the saint "Lazarus". Glenn stands in the middle of this dark "eerie" room as the flames of the candles began to flicker. Glenn turns to the door and standing at the entrance is Benny whom asks, ***"What are you doing here?"***

Glenn shaking hears whispering voices. He turns to the statue of Saint Lazarus and notices behind it a dark figure moving. The candles suddenly blow out! Glenn falls to the floor and Benny rushes towards him. Benny picks up Glenn's head and holds him in his arms. Benny calls out to Glenn, ***"Glenn, Glenn!"***

Suddenly, Glenn opens his eyes and they are rolled back white. Glenn rises out of Benny's arms. He stands in front of him. Glenn's face is pale and demonic looking. He unexpectedly grabs hold of Benny's throat! Benny cries out, ***"Glenn!"***

Glenn smiles. The room fills with screams as the door of the room shuts abruptly with great force!

The phone rings at Karen's mother's house. Karen walks over and picks up saying, ***"Hello?"***

Karen over hears screams and cries on the other end! Then suddenly there is a wicked laugh and the phone goes dead. Karen's mother sitting across her in the living room asks, ***"Who was it?"*** Karen slowly hangs up the phone and turns to her mother saying, ***"Help me turn off all the lights! Forget it I'll do it! Just call the police."***

"What's wrong?" Asks her mother frightened.

Karen walks over to her with the phone and hands it to her saying, ***"Call!"***

Karen's mother takes the phone as Karen turns around walks away to close all windows, check the doors to make sure that they are all locked and shut off all the lights of the house upstairs and downstairs! Karen's mom puts the phone to her ear and notices that the phone has no dial tone: She hangs up and tries again. Still the phone has no dial tone. Karen walks to the kitchen to check the door again and turns off the light as she makes her way towards the living room.

Meanwhile, Dr. Bell is driving towards Benny's house. He is trying to call Karen from the car but the phone is busy. He drives down the streets of Elizabeth rapidly.

Glenn walks out of Benny's house.

Karen asks her mother, ***"Did you get a hold of the police?"*** Karen turns off the last lights as she walks into the living room over to her mother. She sits beside her asking, ***"What? Still no dial tone? Damn cordless phones they're useless!***

"Karen why turn off all the lights?"

As Karen walks over to the front door to make sure it's locked again she says to her mother, ***"If he***

sees the lights on he will see we're home. I don't want to let him know that we are here. Maybe he'll think that we are with Dr. Bell."

"Why is that dangerous?"

"Mom you still don't have the slightest clue of what has been going on. Do you? Hopefully Dr. Bell will find him!

Karen walks back into the darkness of the room and stands beside her mother. Her mother finally gets a dial tone. She dials the number to the police department.

Dr. Bell finally reaches Benny's house with the directions that Karen gave him. He pulls up to the driveway. He sees that the house is dark. He has an empty felling inside. Dr. Bell turns off his car and walks cautiously towards the door. He walks up the steps and rings the doorbell. Within the house shadows twist and turn into form of human bodies. Their heads rattle. They walk behind the darkness whispering and laughing at Benny's brutally murdered body.

Lying in the darkroom upstairs was Benny. He opens his eyes and sees he is surrounded by the high piercing screams of pain. He looks around seeing the horror blinding him by unspeakable acts of violent torture on those who are there with him. He looks up and sees bloody bodies hanging by their ankles crying. He looks down to the ashy ground with his eyes wide open in horror as he sees his mother rising out of the ground! Her eyes are rolled back. Wailing at him, she screams out his name, ***"Benny, mi hijo!"*** (Benny, my son!) She grabs him by his legs and begins to pull him into the earth. Benny struggles! He tries to set himself free from his mother's grasp! She climbs on him pulling him deeper into the ground. Screaming, Benny yells, ***"Mamma!"*** Seeing himself chest deep into the ground, face to face with his mother, she smiles as they sink below the earth! Benny's cries fade!

Dr. Bell opens the door. As he walks in, he feels a dreadful feeling come over him. He stands in the living room, everything was as Benny and Glenn left it. The fire in the fireplace is still burning. Dr. Bell hears raspy breathing sounds coming from upstairs and gasping whispering voices. Dr. Bell slowly walks up the steps. He hears a rasping laugh and a voice says, ***"Satanas!"*** Dr. Bell reaches the top of the stairs, he turns to his right and notices a door wide open with something lying on the ground. Something was standing over it, something big. As Dr. Bell walks towards it, he hears muffled weeps come from the room as he approaches it. He notices that it is Benny's dead body lying on the floor. Standing over him is a large statue of Saint Lazarus. Dr. Bell slowly walks away from the room staring into it with shock he notices the statue's head looking up towards him! He turns and runs down the stairs and out of the house. He quickly gets into his car and drives off! He reaches for his phone inside his coat pocket to call Karen.

The phone is still busy!

Worried and angry, Dr. Bell hopes that Glenn does not think of going to his mother-in-law's house. Especially not in the state of mind he is in! He tries once again to call the house. The line is still busy. Dr. Bell drives quickly towards Karen's mom's house. As he finally approaches the house he sees police cars parked in front of the house. He parks behind one of the patrol cars and rushes into the house! He opens the door and sees that there are cops sitting with Karen's mother but Karen is not there!

A police officer asks Dr. Bell, ***"Excuse me, who are you?"***

Karen walks out of the kitchen with a detective and says, ***"He's my husband's doctor."***

Dr. Bell walks over to where they are and says, ***"Excuse me Detective?"*** To get his name.

"Detective Masa." Responds to the officer.

"Karen excuse what I am about to say. Detective, there has been a murder!"

Karen in shock and in disbelief says, ***"Benny Garcia?"***

The detective calls over three other officers. He turns to Karen and Dr. Bell and asks, ***"What's the address?"***

Karen looks at her mother as her mother walks over to her. Karen hugs her crying in her arms. Dr. Bell gives the address to the detective. As he writes it down he turns to the officers and says, ***"Check it out and report back as soon as possible!"***

As the officers walk out the front door, Karen turns to Dr. Bell and says, ***"The phone rang when you were gone. I knew it was Glenn. I felt it. Whatever was with him, I felt it!"***

With tears in her eyes she sadly continued to say, ***"I can't believe that he killed Benn!"***

As the police officers drive off to Benny's house, Detective Masa tells Karen, ***"I would like to see you***

tomorrow down in the precinct to gather some more information about your husband. Is that all right? Dr. Bell I would like to speak to you as well to see if you can shed some light on some questions I have! Now we definitely have to catch Glenn, before God knows what else he might do next! Here is my number. Call me tomorrow morning and we will talk."

Dr. Bell takes a deep breath and says to himself, ***"God Glenn."***

The following day

It was cold and drizzling. Glenn walks up to St. Catherines Church after walking for hours all night. He is tormented and disoriented. He walks in cold and wet. He walks down the aisle and sits in the middle bench. Glenn closes his eyes trembling. The church is quiet, warm, and peaceful. He opens his eyes and sees crucified upon the cross weeping was Benny! His head was jarring. His skin was pasty white. Glenn's eyes fill with tears. Benny's head stops rattling and he has a smile on his face. His eyes are lifeless and he has a cold look upon his face.

Benny stares at Glenn and says, ***"There is no God here to help you!"***

Benny turns to his right arm and pulls, ripping his hand free from the nails. He turns to his left arm and does the same and also to his feet! His bloody body drops to the floor. Glenn closes his eyes hearing the rasping sound in his head. Benny slowly rises and begins to move walking around the altar dragging his bloody feet as he steps down from it towards Glenn. As he approaches Glenn opens his eyes and notices his face had an evil, wicked expression. Glenn closes and opens his eyes, watching this demonic figure get closer.

Benny spoke out to Glenn asking, ***"You want to be saved?"*** Patronizing Glenn with a smile he asks, ***"Do you?"*** He screams dragging his feet leaving behind a trail of blood. He stands in front of Glenn and leans over facing him face to face. Tears of blood fall from his eyes and he says, ***"Suffer!"*** Glenn closes his eyes. He grows sick from the nauseous smell of rot that surrounds him. Glenn screams out, ***"Leave me alone!"*** He leans forward resting his body on the bench in front of him. Crying he says, ***"I can't take this anymore, I can't!"*** A hand creeps behind him touching his shoulder. Glenn jumps and turns realizing it is Father Thomas!

"I heard someone scream, are you okay Glenn?"

Glenn looks at the crucifix, then looks down to the floor not saying a word.

"You never came to see me!" Says Fr. Thomas.

Glenn looks up to Fr. Thomas with eyes that reflect the trouble of a saddened soul.

"You wanted to see me? Asks Fr. Thomas as he sits next to Glenn.

Glenn speechless stands and walks towards the doors. He says to Fr. Thomas, ***"I believe that there is nothing that can help me Father! All I ask of you is that you pray for me because I need someone like you to pray for me!"***

He walks down towards the doors. Fr. Thomas turns watching him walk away. Before reaching the door Fr. Thomas calls out to him saying, ***"What's wrong? Don't leave!"***

Glenn looks at the door then looks back to Fr. Thomas who is walking towards him. Fr. Thomas's eyes roll back white and blood drips from them as Fr. Thomas says, ***"Don't leave Glenn come!"*** With a smile Glenn turns and walks out the door into the cold rain. Fr. Thomas is puzzled. He watches Glenn walk away through the doors as they slowly close.

Detective Masa and several police officers are at the murder scene. Benny's body was taken late last night. The investigation on Glenn is being followed up with the help of Dr. Bell. He took full responsibility for Glenn. Detective Masa asked him over and over about Glenn's mental history. Dr. Bell is being careful of what he says. Although, knowing that Glenn committed murder he would rather see Glenn under his care in a mental institution, than see him locked up in a penitentiary.

Dr. Bell diagnosed him as a paranoid schizophrenic. Detective Masa walks towards the room where they were. Dr. Bell followed him, answering questions.

"Has he ever shown you any signs of violent behavior, even in his dreams? Asks Det. Masa.

Dr. Bell replies quickly, ***"No, he's not a violent man he.."*** Interrupted by another question from Det. Masa, he asks Dr. Bell, ***"What about his dreams."*** Detective Masa stops and turns to Dr. Bell looking at him saying, ***"You knew that he needed help. A person like him that is so unpredictable should have been committed. Why did you wait? Seems like you doctors like to play around with patients minds!"***

Dr. Bell stood there looking at the bloodstains on the floor. Detective Masa gets on the phone and calls for a county manhunt of Glenn. Listening to

Detective Masa, Dr. Bell knows deep inside that he has to get to Glenn before the police do. He walks across the hall filled with police officers and down the stairs out the front door.

The next day

Karen opens the front door. Just before she steps out she sees a police officer parked across the street. He waves to her. Karen waves back. Karen yells out to her mother, ***"Mom I'm going to the supermarket and the drug store, I'll be back soon!"***

From upstairs her mother answers, ***"Alright dear."***

Karen walks out closing the front door. Karen's mother is up in her bedroom lying in bed with her eyes closed not feeling well. Outside her window, she hears Karen speaking with the police officer parked across the street that is watching the house.

Karen says to the officer, ***"I'm just going to get a couple of things for my mother."***

Karen's mother stands by the window watching Karen get into her car and drive away. The chilly cold winds of winter blow against the window glass. She walks over to her bed and slips back into it closing her eyes. Outside the police officer rolls down his window as another officer passes by. He pulls up along side of him and they begin to chat.

Suddenly, Karen's mother is awakened by a sound coming from downstairs like that of a door opening and then closing. Karen's mom calls out, ***"Karen? You're back so soon?"***

"Yeah mom I'm back." Karen's mother hears her walking up the stairs slowly. A shadow begins to crawl up the wall along the stairs. Karen's mother's face grows faint with fear. She yells, ***"No, No!"*** Her bedroom grows cold. Glenn steps in mimicking Karen's voice. His head rattles.

His voice shaken by the violent jarring of his head says in his own voice, ***"I can't help myself!"*** He walks towards Karen's mother. The door of the room slams violently!

An hour or so passes by. Karen walks in the front door with bags in her arms. She calls out to her mother, ***"Mom, I'm home. Detective Masa and Dr. Bell will be stopping by in a few minutes. I got you cough medicine!"***

As she walks towards the kitchen door she hears, ***"Karen?"*** Her mother's voice calling out to her from upstairs. ***"When you have a chance my love, please bring me a glass of water."***

Karen places the grocery bags upon the table and walks over to the cupboard. She grabs a glass and fills it up with water. As Karen fills the glass she feels something approaching her from behind! She turns and pauses for a moment looking around. There is nothing! She takes the glass of water and walks out the kitchen. Walking up the stairs, the bedroom door slowly opens halfway. Karen notices the door opening. As she reaches the last step, she hears a raspy breathing sound coming from inside the room. Karen slowly walks up to the door as it opens completely! She walks in seeing her mother's lifeless body lying behind the other end of the bed! She drops the glass of water. As it shatters on the floor, she turns and looks over to the bed. Sitting on it with his legs crossed is Glenn. His head and body are covered with a bed sheet. He speaks out to her in her mother's voice but in a strange language. Karen is terrified. She is paralyzed with fear as her eyes fill with tears. She wants to run out the room, but she is completely numb! She can't react! She can't even scream!

Glenn slowly pulls the bed sheet off his head. His eyes are rolled back white and he has a cynical smirk on his face. He slowly gets off the bed with a knife in his hand. He walks towards Karen as he breathes in with a heavy rasping sound. Karen snaps out of it and runs out of the room towards the stairs! Glenn runs after her. He cries out a painful scream. Karen runs down the steps. She notices a figure of a person dressed in black with a hood over its head kneeling at the front door! It is hitting its head against the door pounding it harder and harder! Karen looks up at the top of the stairs. Glenn walks behind her down the steps. She leaps over the banister and falls hitting the floor! In pain with a broken leg, she drags herself into the living room. She pauses and notices dark figures with black hoods on their heads facing the wall. They smash their heads against the wall surrounding her. She turns around and her eyes are wide open with terror as Glenn stands over her! Outside the house, parking his car is Dr. Bell with Detective Masa.

Karen releases a scream but no sound comes from her! Dr. Bell and Detective Masa can't hear her. Dr. Bell opens the car door and steps out closing the door behind him. He looks at the house. Detective Masa walks towards him as Dr. Bell stares at the house. He begins to walk towards it faster and faster! Detective Masa follows him. They finally hear Karen's cries. They rush up to the door and Dr. Bell yells out, ***"Karen!"*** Detective Masa pushes Dr. Bell aside and with all his strength slams his body into the door trying to break in!

Glenn has a knife. He raises it. The dark figures pound their heads harder and faster against the walls. Glenn savagely stabs Karen's hopeless body! Detective Masa shoots at the door lock and finally breaks in! The dark figures fade away! The front door slams wide open. Detective Masa holds up his gun pointing it at Glenn yelling, ***"Glenn!"*** Glenn turns around holding Karen's lifeless body by her hair. Dr. Bell runs in behind Detective Masa. He is blinded by the horror he sees. He covers his eyes. Glenn steps back, dropping the bloody knife, as it falls onto the pool of blood. He looks around hearing laughter all around him.

A few weeks later

After an investigation, Glenn's lawyer enters a plea of insanity on his behalf. Dr. Bell petitions the court so that Glenn is placed in his custody. The judge grants Dr. Bell custody of Glenn saying, ***"I will grant that Glenn be put in your care! But he is to spend the remainder of his days in the institution with no hope of parole..."*** Glenn lifts his head. His hands are upon his face. He sobs in grief. The courtroom blackens.

Days, weeks pass. Glenn is inside his cell surrounded by others who suffer as well. Sitting in a dark corner of the room, it fills with whispering voices. Glenn rocks himself back and forth with his head down. Exhausted, he hears next to him on the other side of the cell wall a voice. Glenn lifts his head resting it on the wall beside him silently weeping, as he listens...

In a bright white room dressed in white, there is a young man writing on the wall. His eyes are exhausted and swollen by his constant tears. He has dark bags underneath his eyes. He turns to look behind him at the door of his room as he stops writing. He slowly walks across the room towards the door to peek through a small glass window. His eyes open wide wandering around the room you can see his face reflecting the little sanity that is left in his mind. He hears loud tormented moans approaching rapidly from far down the dark hall. The young man slowly steps away from the door where he can hear the suffering, frightening horrible cries coming from the other side. The young man turns around, walks back to the wall where he bends down and picks up a black marker on the floor. As he stands turning to the door he says to himself, (softly biting his fingernails), ***"They're out there but they're not coming yet, I still have time!"*** He smiles. He then turns to the wall and begins to write as he whispers word for word what he's writing on the wall.

He writes, **The sands of time slowly slip between my fingers as night falls upon me I feel myself drowning slowly deep into a spell within me. My mind no longer belongs to me. People do not have the capacity to comprehend the torture that I have to live with every day of my goddamn life. Writing on this wall is the only way that I can explain to whomever reads this, what I am feeling.**

The young man pauses and slowly turns back to the door as he hears them calling out to him, ***"Thomas."*** He turns back to the wall.

Outside the door he hears laughter. He continues to write **I don't know what these things want with me. Am I crazy? I am lost in this maze called a brain. But I know what I see, feel, and hear can't be madness. My body witnesses the tortures that I have to live with everyday of fuck'n life. I'm locked inside in my own nightmare and I can't wake from it. I scream but no one hears me. These demons that I see, they laugh at me when I cry. I can't stand the pain that I feel!"**

The young man looks back to the door and walks to the next wall. He lifts his arm to write and a voice whispers next to his ear, ***"Hell waits for you Thomas, nothing can save you not even God!"***

Thomas weeps like a frightened child. He releases a low sigh. He closes his eyes as he sobs. He opens his eyes looks up to the wall and continues to write, **I lift my eyes to the ceiling, close them and imagine that I'm looking up to a night sky. I see stars shining in the blackness. I see them fall from grace. As they fall, they fall with screams disappearing into the dark abyss. I can feel the cold chills of those who fear to sleep, my tongue and my lips can taste the tears of those who burn in their own Hell. My destiny, please release me from this hell, I can feel them right now outside my door drawing near. I hear them.**

The small glass window of the door cracks and is followed by a gasping sound. Thomas looks at the door. His face grows weary. He slowly walks to the door. The door slowly opens Thomas stops. The room behind him darkens as the hall slowly lights up brightly, as if there was a light shining down from heaven. There, standing outside his door is a beautiful white horse and behind it is pure darkness. Within the darkness there are some figures moving. Thomas tries to see what is moving behind the horse but he can't quite make out what it is. He dares to take a step forward towards the horse! A gasping voice calls out to him, ***"Thomas."***

Suddenly out of no where demons jump on the horse. The door slams shut the light of the room begins to flicker. Thomas steps back until his back is against the wall in the cell. He covers his ears to block out the sound of the hopeless animal being tortured! The poor horse is being ripped to shreds as the demons feast on the frenzy! Thomas opens his eyes and he notices the silence surrounding him. He slowly uncovers his ears, looks up to the door and notices the blood on the door window! He looks down and sees the blood slowly flowing underneath the door. Thomas looks up from the wall towards the bloody window, a ghoulish demonic face yells at him, ***"Your hell will be unimaginable!"*** Their laughter echoes around him. Then suddenly, there is silence again. Thomas slowly gets up from the floor, turns to the wall where his writing is and leans his head against it. He whispers to himself, ***"Why? What have I done?"***

The room grows cold. Mist comes out of his mouth as he breaths deeply looking back at the door. Thomas looks down to the floor, bends over and picks up his black marker. He turns to the wall and continues writing, **I pray that God will take me**

away before they do, I can't live like this, in this hell!

A voice whispers into his ears, ***"You don't know what Hell is!"***

Thomas's eyes fill with tears. He continues writing, **God save me, God save me!**

He stops writing and turns his head. Outside the door down towards the dark hall, something walks slowly towards his cell. Thomas peeks through the cell door window and sees the other patient's doors suddenly swing open! He can see others being dragged from their rooms by their temples with large rusty hooks being pulled by chains. Demons drag these poor souls as they scream out in pain. The demons lift their bodies up in the air as they cry. Within Thomas's room, the light begins to flicker once again. Thomas turns and looks at the flickering lights. He turns to look out the window. There is nothing, just an empty hall! There is no screaming, no patients. There was only a quiet dark hall!

"Thomas", he hears behind him a gasping voice. He turns, there sitting in a corner of the cell is a pale young woman in a straight jacket. Her skin is pasty, her lips have no color and her eyes are closed. She says to him, ***"Thomas why did you let them take me?"***

He replies, ***"You became one of them!"***

"Became what?" She opens her eyes they roll back white. She gets up from the floor and quickly walks over to Thomas repeating over and over again, ***"They are coming Thomas, they are coming!"***

The room began to spin around him as his wife (the young woman) began to laugh at him. He falls to the floor. Thomas covering his ears yells, ***"I'm***

sorry I couldn't do anything. I had to kill you. You became one of them.." Crying on the floor Thomas lay there until morning came.

The sun shined through the windows of the dark hall as the light shined through the cracks into the window of the door of Thomas's cell. Thomas awakened by a knocking sound opens his eyes. He looks around slowly. He sits up and looks towards the door where he hears, ***"You wrote on the wall again ha Mr. Thomas?"*** Thomas looks up to the wall and looks down to the floor. He does not say a word. The formerly says cruelly, ***"Here, now take your medicine."*** Thomas walks over to the door. The small slot on the door opens, he takes his pills and a small cup of water. As he takes his medication, he looks through the small opening in the door and stares at the formerly. He then swallows the pills and hands the cup back to the formerly smiling. The formerly angrily leans forward and says, ***"Stand back in your corner we have to transfer you to another room because it's clean up time!"***

Thomas walks to his corner. The formerly walks in and straps him up in a straight jacket. Dr. Iglesias walks in (Thomas's psychiatrist) and says, ***"Hello Mr. Sans."*** He looks around the cell and walks to where the walls are written on by Thomas. He stands reading what Thomas has written saying, ***"This is what you experienced last night Mr. Sans?"***

Thomas looks up at Dr. Iglesias and speaks not a word.

"I told you many times, many, many times that all these things that you say you hear, see and feel are all

in your head! Mr. Johnson take Mr. Sans to his new room."

The formerly takes Thomas out the cell and walks him down the hall. The other patient's doors were open as Thomas passed them by. Thomas glances into one of the cells, his eyes open with fear as he notices one of the patient's heads rattling! The patient reaches out crying softly, ***"Help me!"***

He passes another cell and sees a patient sitting on his bed in a straight jacket. His face shows demonic possession as his eyes roll back into his head, laughing saying, ***"Tonight Thomas we come for you!"*** The patient screams out saying, ***"Save me from them, save me!"***

Thomas begins to cry out loud, ***"No God no!"***

Thomas struggles in the formerly's arms as he tried to drag him down the hall into his new cell. He was hysterical. He finally dragged him in. He pushed Thomas. As he walked out the cell he slams the doors behind him. He lies on the floor weeping, where he finally falls asleep.

Hours pass by and the night sets in. The cold October winds blew making the sound of hungry wolves crying. Thomas was awakened by a loud bang as he quickly sits up and drags himself against the wall. He stares at the door. He hears rasping sounds behind it as the light of his room shuts off. He sits in the dark as he hears in the hall painful moans. Thomas, struggling to get up on his knees against the wall hears a gasping voice call out to him, ***"Thomas."*** He eventually gets up on his feet and slowly walks to the door where he once again hears the gasping voice calling out to him. An asthmatic laugh follows behind it as he looks out the small glass window. He looks down deep into the darkness of the hall where slowly creeping out of the black darkness is a fog like vapor flowing towards his cell. There are whispering voices accompanied with excruciating tormenting cries as the doors of the other patients cells open. Out from them come screams! Thomas's room begins to grow colder. The black fog draws closer. The whispering voices softly murmur, ***"Satanas."*** The whispering voice begins to speak in a strange language. The light of his room begins to flicker on and off. Thomas turns and looks at it as he looks out the window of the door onto the floor. Within the darkness of the fog there slowly appears clearly out of the mist ghoulish demons crawling and dragging themselves. They moan, cry and say, ***"Thomas we will feast upon your remains, we are coming for you!"***

From inside the room Thomas hears monstrous animal-like growls. Thomas turns with terror, as his eyes open wide with panic. Suddenly, something picks him up and throws him across the cell. His body hits the wall and falls to the floor. Quickly, in pain he drags himself to a corner. Inside with him he hears whispering voices all around him. He feels something touching him. He feels their presence in the room. He tries to move away but something will not let him. The lights go out. Thomas sees himself sitting in the dark. He looks at the door and notices the crack underneath. He sees the shadows of those things, crawling to the door. He hears the raspy breathing as the fog slowly reaches the door and creeps in underneath filling the room. The door swings open. Dark human like shadows walk in the cell. Their heads jar violently. The dark mist moves towards Thomas and a voice says, ***"It's time Thomas!"***

The door closes. You hear Thomas weeping, ***"Let this all end already!"***

The door slowly opens from within the dark mist where the demonic ghouls rise and stand in the middle of the cell. The door begins to close and open repeatedly. Each time it closes the slamming sound grows louder and louder. Thomas is surrounded by the darkness of the room. He notices rising from the floor arms reaching out to him. They grab Thomas on his knees, he screams, ***"Someone save me!"*** A chain shoots out of the mist, wraps itself around Thomas's neck pulling him to the floor into the fog. The door still repeatedly opens and closes, then stops.

Slowly, the door creaks open. Thomas struggles! He can't set himself free. He's in a straight jacket and the chain begins to tighten around his neck! They drag him out the cell. The demonic human like ghouls turn and slowly walk out the room behind him. They lean over and drop to their knees. Their heads lift up as they transform into vapor. Thomas sits up within the fog. His eyes fill with tears as the chain wrapped around his neck extends into the darkness of the hall. Thomas hears a voice talking. He turns to his right and sees Dr. Iglesias and two other nurses at the end of the hall. He tries to scream but he can't! No sound comes out from his mouth. As they walk away, he tries repeatedly to scream! Still no sound comes from him. Thomas looks away and closes his eyes. Tears fall from them. He opens them and looks down to the floor.

The howling wind intensifies as the gentle rattling sound of the chain wraps around his neck echoing down the dark hall! Thomas slowly looks up and sees a tall dark figure standing in front of him. The chain wrapped around his neck yanks him, dragging his body down into the mist. It pulls him like he was a piece of meat down the dark hall into the blackness. The hall echoes with sounds of his body being hauled. Turning back, one can see Thomas's lonely dark cell empty.

Looking deep into it, you hear multiple whispering voices. Within the voices, you hear a rasping chuckle. A growling sound grows in the dark cell. The door slams shut violently!

Two doors down is Glenn hitting his head against the glass window of the door. His eyes roll back white with a wicked smile as he says softly, ***"If there is a God save me, save me, someone save me!"***

Half way down the hall a security guard hears a banging sound. He looks up. Glenn stops banging his head against the window and stares back at the security guard. Tears fall from Glenn's eyes as tormenting cries fill his room! He slowly steps back into the darkness of the cell. Hearing screams Glenn weeps....

"Peace to those who suffer"

Dr. Bell walks into Glenn's study. As he looks around the room his eyes notice a book that is opened lying on the desk. He walks towards it, pulls the chair towards him. He sits and begins to read what the book contains. He realizes that it's Glenn's journal.

He reads on…

I walk these city streets. The torment in my mind drives me to believe was I really born to suffer? As I walk, images of my life slowly fade to black. My life is no longer life. My mind is no longer mine! I don't even own a piece of sanity! Why, I don't even know why I'm living in this dark spell. Slowly day by day, life turns into a living hell. Reality doesn't matter anymore. Time is ticking away and there's no end to what I feel. All of this is just one bad dream. I scream. Can anyone hear me? All I want is to wake up, but this dream has no end to it. Good things come to those who wait, "Not true!" I dream of a world that has lost its meaning in my life. I can't remember the last time I had a sweet dream. These dark creatures rape my mind. I don't believe in angels or demons but these things that stare back at me find pleasure in torturing me! They call out to me. I hear screams. I hear whispering voices. You may say, "I am crazy." I am not sick. Believe me when I say, "I'm not, I'm not crazy! Don't cast me away. I hurt! I suffer! Am I trapped in my own mind? Or am I a voice screaming out in my head, ***"This is reality!"***

Salvate! Save yourself!

I see myself battle my demons that desire to twist my world. They sink my mind into a pit of slavery. I wake up everyday with a prayer and sleep holding onto God's robe.

When I see the dark clouds form over my head and I see no sun for days my soul cries out for peace. I sit in the dark thinking of a way out of this that surrounds me, madness!

They sit before me, pointing at me, pointing out my tears as they laugh tormenting me. I stay strong within the darkness and all the insanity growing around me. I begin to notice behind my tormentor, behind the dark images I see a light, a gentle light! What seems to take form of a candle, the flames grow making the dark eerie room brighten with light. The black images sitting before me quickly stand screaming. Blinded, hiding in the dark corners of the room, angry, they stare at me. They wait until the flames of the candle die out so they can do their will. Until then, I rest my mind and enjoy in relief the warmth of the light of the candle flame…

TICK, TOCK,TICK, TOCK, time escapes between my fingers. I close my eyes and lift my head towards the wind as it gently caresses my face like hands. I hear a voice speak, ***"tomorrow never."*** I look up to the night sky I see them hiding behind the stars laughing at me. I close my eyes. All I wish and all that I desire is that I want them to give me what is rightfully mine, my mind. I lay in green pastures hidden deep in the high grass. They pass me by like jackals hunting for their prey. Deep inside I pray, ***"let me see another day."*** I know things that can only come from nightmares are chasing me. Animals of a dark half of my mind, these things feed on tears and pain, harvesters of torture. I lay still, quiet. I slowly release my breath not fast all at once, breath by breath reassuring myself that I will see another day out of hell...

TAPPING THE VEIN OF THIS WORLD TRYING TO FIND A WAY OUT. TAPPING THE VEIN OF REALITY SOMETIMES I CAN'T TELL IF I AM ASLEEP OR AWAKE. MY DREAMS IF THEY ARE DREAMS, BECOME DARKER AND DARKER, UNTIL I AM BLIND. BLIND THAT I CAN NOT TELL WHAT IS REALITY. WHAT SURROUNDS ME IS IT REAL?

TAPPING THE VEIN OF MY LIFE. MY LIFE IS A MAZE. I AM LOST. I CAN'T FIND THE WAY OUT. FRUSTRATING? IS IT WHEN YOU GO IN CIRCLES ROUND AND ROUND RUNNING CONFUSED LOOKING FOR A WAY OUT? SCARED OUT OF YOUR MIND. KEEP ASKING YOURSELF AM I ASLEEP? AM I JUST DREAMING? SOON I WILL WAKE UP

AND ALL THIS WILL JUST BE A BAD DREAM. IT IS JUST IN MY HEAD. STRESS, THAT'S WHAT IT IS, STRESS.

TIME PASSES BY, YOU DON'T WAKE UP HEARING THINGS, VOICES IN YOUR HEAD THAT TORMENT YOU. I TRY TO FIND MYSELF BUT THE PATH TO REALITY IS TO FREEDOM OF THE MIND. IT JUST BECAME DARK, FADING INTO THE MIST. I STOP TO GATHER MY THOUGHTS. I BEGIN TO LAUGH. MY LAUGHTER BECOMES CRIES. I CRY OUT, ***"RELEASE ME!"*** IN MY EARS, I HEAR A VOICE WHISPER SOFTLY, ***"NEVER."***

GLENN...

I fear the things that fill my life with terror. The grace of God has abandoned me. I am alone. My mind is filled with laughter that brings me down to my knees. This madness, this dark curse that damns me to be a slave to this Hell that I call my life. I cry out for angels to rescue me but all I see are demons tormenting me. This sadness sinks me deep into the cold dark waters of pain. I am drowning. I feel them pulling me under. I struggle to set myself free from their grasp and swim for the shores of despair. Tired and weak I feel that I am being nipped at my body. I have no voice. I have no strength to fight off these dogs that chase after my soul. I have the chance to get away for now. Nevertheless, I look back at my footprints. Slowly they fade away leaving no trace for anyone to find me. I am lost. I look up gazing to the dark skies. Searching for light to illuminate my steps in this dark world. I see not one star, they all have fallen just like me, fallen. They are forgotten, burned away just like me, like my life slowly falling into

Darkness…

Darkness falls upon me. Heaven cries, the tears of angels fall on my skin. I feel the fear inside me grow like weeds. The moon, the only light that shines its grace. Light for my eyes to see. I close them not wanting to witness the images that stand before me. Feeling their unpleasant presence I feel them creeping around me. Trembling with fear the silence becomes frightening. I sob in the darkness as the light of the moon slowly fades to black. I hear their laughter. I glance up to the dark sky and see an eclipse. The moon light dies. I am in a place that my mind seems to be trapped in. I do not want to be in the dark anymore. I pray that I can see light again…

Have you ever seen yourself surrounded by demons twisting your life with every plea that you make for them to stop? But the truth of this sour reality is that they find pleasure seeing me break down as my life spins round and round. I find myself lost in a world that my mind can not find its way out. I am drowning in sorrow, hurting for peace, peace of mind to release me from a hell that unleashes its fury on me. Yes, I feel forsaken in a world that has no idea what I am going through. My voice does not reach the heaven. My tears are ignored but God does not know why. I only know that I find myself in Hell. My eyes are so, so tired of expressing a soul that fears it is lost. A soul that wants to be set free, free from its

Demons…

Oh God almighty, save me from these tormentors that enslave me in this madness. I can not set myself free. My life is filled with sorrow. My days are dark. Help me, rescue me. I plead to you, my heart bleeds in anguish. I am blinded by the terror that surrounds me. My body is battered and weak. Today is a day of suffering. I fear what tomorrow can bring. My world is falling apart. I lost complete grasp of reality. I am so tired of tasting tears. Heaven, do not forsake me. Shine your grace upon me. I find myself in darkness. It seems all my prayers are hopeless. I feel them drawing near. Soon madness will begin…

HENRY DAVID THOREAU
1817-1862
**"BE IT LIFE OR DEATH,
WE CRAVE ONLY REALITY."**

About The Author

Dauzed Melgarejo, Jr. is a published Cuban-American poet and author of several short stories and novels. One particular poem is *"Quest for Peace"*, found in The International Library of Poetry. *Infernal* is a highly regarded novel that will appeal to the fans of classical horror. He wants to draw people to experience the ultimate feeling of terror as they read this horrifying story of what evil truly is!

Raised in a family of artists (writers, musicians, painters, and an elite fashion designer), Dauzed's life has been enriched by many talents. He is currently involved in enhancing his education in communications in film and screenwriting in hopes to one day co-produce the film version of this novel.

He lives in Central New Jersey with his wife.

Printed in the United States
998100001B